Anting-Anting Stories

Sargent Kayme

Contents

ANTING-ANTING STORIES

BY

Sargent Kayme

FOREWORD

The life of the inhabitants of the far-away Eastern islands in which the people of the United States are now so vitally interested opens to our literature a new field not less fresh and original than that which came to us when Mr. Kipling first published his Indian tales. India had always possessed its wonders and its remarkable types, but they waited long for adequate expression. No less wonderful and varied are the inhabitants and the phenomena of the Philippines, and a new author, showing rare knowledge of the country and its strange peoples, now gives us a collection of simple yet powerful stories which bring them before us with dramatic vividness.

Pirates, half naked natives, pearls, man-apes, towering volcanoes about whose summits clouds and unearthly traditions float together, strange animals and birds, and stranger men, pythons, bejuco ropes stained with human blood, feathering palm trees now fanned by soft breezes and now crushed to the ground by tornadoes;--on no mimic stage was ever a more wonderful scene set for such a company of actors. That the truly remarkable stories written by Sargent Kayme do not exaggerate the realities of this strange life can be easily seen by any one who has read the letters from press correspondents, our soldiers, or the more formal books of travel.

Strangest, perhaps, of all these possibilities for fiction is the anting-anting, at once a mysterious power to protect its possessor and the outward symbol of the protection. No more curious fetich can be found in the history of folk-lore. A button, a coin, a bit of paper with unintelligible words scribbled upon it, a bone, a stone, a garment, anything, almost--often a thing of no intrinsic value--its owner has been known to walk up to the muzzle of a loaded musket or rush upon the point of a bayonet with a confidence so sublime as to silence ridicule and to command admiration if not respect.

THE ANTING-ANTING OF CAPTAIN VON TOLLIG

There had been a battle between the American forces and the Tagalogs, and the natives had been driven back. The stone church of Santa Maria, around which the engagement had been hottest, and far beyond which the native lines had now been driven, had been turned into a hospital for the wounded Tagalogs left by their comrades on the field. Beneath a broad thatched shed behind the church lay the bodies of the dead, stiff and still under the coverings of cocoanut-fibre cloth thrown hastily over them. The light of a full tropic moon threw the shadow of the roof over them like a soft, brown velvet pall. They were to be buried between day-break and sunrise, that the men who buried them might escape the heat of the day.

The American picket lines had been posted a quarter of a mile beyond the church, near which no other guards had been placed. Not long after midnight a surgeon, one of the two men left on duty in the church, happened to look out through a broken window towards the shed, and in the shadow, against the open moonlight-flooded field beyond, saw something moving. Looking close he could make out the slim, brown figure of a native passing swiftly from one covered form to another, and turning back the cocoanut-fibre cloth to look at each dead man's face.

Calling the man who was working with him the surgeon pointed out the man beneath the shed to him. "That fellow has no business there," he said, "He has slipped through the lines in some way. He may be a spy, but even if he is not, he is here for no good. We must capture him."

"All right," was the answer. "You go around the church one way, and I will come the other."

When the surgeon, outside the hospital, reached a place where he could see the shed again, the Tagalog had ceased his search. He had found the body he was looking for, and sunk down on his knees beside it was searching for something in the clothing which covered the dead man's breast. A moment later he had seen the men stealing towards him from the church, had cleared the open space beneath the shed at a leap, and was off in the moonlight, running towards the outposts. The surgeons swore; and one fired a shot after him from his revolver.

"Might as well shoot at the shadow of that palm tree," the one who had shot said. "Anyway it will wake up the pickets, and they may catch him.

"What do you suppose he was after?" he added.

"Don't know," said his companion. "You wait, and I'll get a lantern and we will see."

The lantern's light showed the clothing parted over a dead man's body, and the fragment of a leather thong which had gone about his neck, with broken ends. Whatever had been fastened to the thong was gone, carried away by the Tagalog when he had fled.

The next morning a prisoner was brought to headquarters. "The picket who caught him, sir," the officer who brought the prisoner reported, "said he heard a shot near the church where the wounded natives are; and then this man came running from that way."

The surgeons who had been on night duty at the hospital were sent for, and their story heard.

"Search the man," said the officer in command.

The native submitted to the ordeal in sullen silence, and made no protest, when, from some place within his clothing, there was taken a small, dirty leather bag from which two broken ends of leather thong still hung. Only his eyes followed the officer's hands wolfishly, as they untied the string which fastened the bag, and took from it a little leather-bound book not more than two inches square. The officer looked at the book curiously. It was very thin, and upon the tiny pages, yellow with age, there was writing, still legible, although the years which had stained the paper yellow had faded the ink. He spelled out a few words, but they were in a language which he did not know. "Take the man to the prison," he said. "I will keep the book."

Later in the day the officer called an orderly. "Send Lieutenant Smith to me," he said.

By one of the odd chances of a war where, like that in the Philippines, the forces at first must be hastily raised, Captain Von Tollig and the subordinate officer for whom he had sent, had been citizens of the same town. The captain had been a business man, shrewd and keen,--too keen some of his neighbors sometimes said of him. Lieutenant Smith was a college man, a law student. It had been said of them in their native town that both had paid court to the same young woman, and that the younger man had won in the race. If this were so, there had been no evidence on the part of either in the service to show that they were conscious of the fact. There had been little communication between them, it is true, but when there had been the subordinate officer never overlooked the deference due his superior.

"I wish you would take this book," said Captain Von Tollig, after he had told briefly how the volume happened to be in his possession, "and see if you can translate it. I suspect it must be something of value, from the risk this man took to get it; possibly dispatches from one native leader to another, the nature of which we ought to know."

The young man took the queer little book and turned the pages curiously. "I hardly think what is written here can be dispatches," he said, "The paper and the ink both look too old for that. The words seem to be Latin; bad Latin, too, I should say. I think it is what the natives call an 'anting-anting;' that is a charm of some kind. Evidently this one did not save the life of the man who wore it. Probably it is a very famous talisman, else they would not have run such a risk to try to get it back."

"Can you read it?"

"Not off hand. With your permission I will take it to my tent, and I think I can study it out there."

"Do so. When you make English of it I'd like to know what it says. I am getting interested in it"

The lieutenant bowed, and went away.

"Bring that prisoner to me," the captain ordered, later in the day.

"Do you want to go free?" he asked, when the Tagalog had been brought.

"If the Senor wills."

"What is that book?"

The man made no answer.

"Tell me what the book is, and why you wanted it; and you may go home."

"Will the Senor give me back the book to carry home with me?"

"I don't know. I'll see later about that."

"It was an 'anting-anting.' The strongest we ever knew. The man who had it was a chief. When he was dead I wanted it."

"If this was such a powerful charm why was the man killed who had it on. Why didn't it save him?"

The Tagalog was silent.

"Come. Tell me that, and you may go."

"And have the book?"

"Yes; and have the book."

"It is a very great 'anting-anting.' It never fails in its time. The man who made it, a famous wise man, very many years ago, watched one whole month for the secrets which the stars told him to write in it; but the last night, the night of the full moon, he fell asleep, and on that one day and night of the month the 'anting-anting' has no good in it for the man who wears it. Else the chief would not be dead. You made the attack, that day. Our people never would."

"Lieutenant Smith to see you, sir," an orderly announced.

"All right. Send him in; and take this fellow outside."

"But, Senor," the man's eyes plead for him as loudly as his words; "the 'anting-anting.' You said I could have it and go."

"Yes, I know. Go out and wait."

"What do you report, Lieutenant? Can you read it?"

"Yes. This is very singular. There is no doubt but the book is now nothing but a charm."

"Yes. I found that out."

"But I feel sure it was originally something more than that. Something very strange."

"What?"

"It purports to be the record of the doings of a man who seems to have died here many years ago, written by himself. It tells a strange story, which, if true, may be of great importance now. To make sure the record would be kept the writer made the natives believe it was a charm, while its being written in Latin kept the nature of its message from them."

"Have you read it?"

"Most of it. Sometimes a word is gone--faded out;--and a few words I cannot translate;--I don't remember all my Latin. I have written out a translation as nearly as I can make it out." He handed a paper to the captain, who read:

"I, Christopher Lunez, am about to die. Once I had not thought that this would be my end,--a tropic island, with only savages about me. I had thought of something very different, since I got the gold. Perhaps, after all, there is a curse on treasure got as that was. If there is, and the sin is to be expiated in another world, I shall know it soon. I did not--"

Here there was a break, and the story went on.

"---- all the others are dead, and the wreck of our ship has broken to bits and has disappeared. Before the ruin was complete, though, I had brought the gold on shore and buried it. No one saw me. The natives ran from us at first, far into the forest, and ----"

The words which would have finished the sentence were wanting.

"Where three islands lie out at sea in a line with a promontory like a buffalo's head, I sunk the gold deep in the sands, at the foot of the cliff, and dug a rude cross in the rock above it. Some day I hope a white man guided by this, will find the treasure and--"

"There was no more," said the lieutenant, when the captain, coming to this sudden end looked up at him. "The last few pages of the book are gone, torn out, or worn loose and lost. What I have translated was scattered over many pages, with disconnected signs and characters written in between. The book was evidently intended to be looked upon as a mystic talisman, probably that the natives on this account might be sure to take good care of it.

"All of the Tagalogs who can procure them, carry these 'anting-anting.' Some are thought to be much more powerful than others. Evidently this was looked upon as an unusually valuable charm. Sometimes they are only a button, sewed up in a rag. One of the prisoners we took not long ago wore a broad piece of cloth over his breast, on which was stained a picture of a man killing another with a 'barong.' He believed that while he wore it no one could kill him with that weapon; and thought the only reason he was not killed in the skirmish in which he was captured was because he had the 'anting-anting' on."

"Do you believe the story which the book tells is true?" the captain inquired.

"I don't know. Some days I think I could believe anything about this country."

"Have you shown the book to any one else, or told any one what you make out of it?"

"No."

"Do not do so, then. That is all, now. I will keep the book," he added, putting the little brown volume inside his coat.

Several days later the officer in charge of the quarters where the native prisoners were confined reported to the captain: "One of the prisoners keeps begging to be allowed to see you, sir," he said. "He says you told him he might go free. Shall I let him be brought up here?"

"Yes. Send him up."

"Well?" said Captain Von Tollig, when the man appeared at headquarters, and the orderly who had brought him had retired.

"The little book, Senor. You said I could have it back, and go."

"Yes. You may go. I will have you sent safely through our lines; but the book I have decided to keep."

The man's face grew ash-colored with disappointment or anger. "But, Senor," he protested. "You told me ----"

"I know; but I have changed my mind. You can go, if you wish, without the book, or not, just as you choose."

"Then I will stay," the Tagalog said slowly, adding a moment later, "My people will surely slay me if I go back to them without the book."

"Very well." The captain called for the guard, and the man was taken back to prison; but later in the day an order was sent that he be released from confinement and put to work with some other captured natives about the camp.

During the next two or three weeks a stranger to Tagalog methods of warfare might very reasonably have thought the war was ended, so far as this island, at least, was concerned. The natives seemed to have disappeared mysteriously. Even the men who had been longest in the service were puzzled to account for the sudden ceasing of the constant skirmishing which had been the rule before. The picket lines were carried forward and the location of the camp followed, from time to time, as scouting parties returned to report the country clear of foes. The advance would have been even more rapid, except for the necessity of keeping communication open at the rear with the harbour where two American gunboats lay at anchor.

As a result of one of the advances the camp was pitched one night upon a broad plateau looking out upon the sea. Inland the ground rose to the thickly forest-clad slope of a mountain, to which the American officers felt sure the Tagalogs had finally retreated. Early in the evening, when the heat of the day had passed, a group of these officers were standing with Captain Von Tollig in the center of the camp, examining the mountain slope with their glasses.

"What did you say was the name of this place?" one of the officers asked a native deserter who had joined the American forces, and at times had served as a guide to the expedition.

"That is Mt. Togonda," he answered, pointing to the hills before them, "and this," swinging his hand around the plateau on which the camp's tents were pitched, "is La Plaza del Carabaos."

The captain's eyes met those of Lieutenant Smith.

"La Plaza del Carabaos" means "The Square of the Water Buffalos."

As if with one thought the two men turned and looked out to sea. The sun had set. Against the glowing western sky a huge rock at the plateau's farthest limit was outlined. Rough-carved as the rock had been by the chisel of nature, the likeness to a water buffalo's head was striking. Beyond the rock three islands lay in a line upon the sunset-lighted water. Far out from the foot of the cliff the two men could hear the waves beating upon the sand.

"This is an excellent place for a camp," the captain said when he turned to his men again. "I think we shall find it best to stay here for some time."

Perhaps a month of respite from attack had made the sentries careless; perhaps it was only that the Tagalogs had spent the time in gathering strength. No one can ever know just how that wicked slaughter of our soldiers in the campaign on that island did come about.

The Tagalogs swept down into the camp that night as a hurricane might have blown the leaves of the mountain trees across the plateau; and then were gone again, leaving death, and wounds worse than death, behind them.

When our men had rallied, and had come back across the battle-ground, they found among the others, the captain lying dead outside his tent. A Tagalog dagger lay beside the body, and the uniform had been torn apart until the officer's bare breast showed.

The first full moon of the month shone down upon the dead man's white, still face.

THE CAVE IN THE SIDE OF CORON

A"barong" is a Moro native's favourite weapon. With one deft whirl, and then a downward slash of the keen steel blade he can cleave the skull of an opponent from crown to teeth, or cut an arm clean from the shoulder socket.

When I was sent with a squad of brave men from my company to reconnoitre from Mt. Halcon, in the Island of Mindoro, and the force was ambushed, the way I saw the men meet death will always make me hate a Moro. Why I was spared, then, and bound, instead of being killed like the men, I could not imagine. Later I knew.

The Moros had no business to be on Mindoro, anyway. Their home was in Mindanao, far to the south, but three hundred years of Spanish attempt to rule them had left them still an untamed people, and the war between the two races had been endless. Each year when the southwest monsoons had blown, the Moro war-proas had gone northward carrying murder and pillage wherever they had appeared. When the Spanish were not too much occupied elsewhere they fitted out retaliatory expeditions which left effects of little permanence. That year the Moros had found not Spaniards but a small force of American troops, sent south from Manila, and from them had cut off my little scouting squad. It made no difference to them that we were of another nation. They cared nothing for a change in rulers. We were white, and Christians; that was enough. We were to be slain.

The leader of the Moros was a tall old man with glittering eyes set in a gloomy face. I watched him as I lay bound on the deck of one of the war-proas; for, fearing attack I suppose, soon after my capture the sails had been spread and the fleet of boats turned to the south.

"Feed him" the chief had said, when night came on, and pointed to me with his foot. I thought then I had been saved from death for slavery, and deemed that the worst fate possible, I did not know the Moro nature.

On the afternoon of the fifth day out, we passed Busuanga and approached a small rocky island which I afterwards learned was Coron. So far as could be seen no human habitation was near, and far to the south stretched the unbroken waters of the Sulu Sea. The chief gave an order in the Moro tongue, and a black and yellow flag was run up to the mast head. In response to the signal all the proas of the fleet joined us in a little bay at the end of the island, and dropped anchor. At one side of the bay it would be possible to land and climb from there to the top of the island, from which, everywhere else, as far as I could see, a sheer cliff came down three hundred feet to where the waves beat against the jagged rocks at its base.

The smaller boats which had been towed behind the larger craft were cast off and brought alongside the chief's proa. I was lifted into one and rowed to a place where we could land. My feet had been untied, but my hands were still fastened behind my back. Two Moros grasped me by the arms and guided me between them. They would not let me turn my head, but I could hear the voices of men following us. The chief led the way. He did not speak or pause until we had reached the level summit of the island. When he did speak it was in Spanish, which he had learned that I understood. We were halted on the very edge of the precipice. Far down below the little fleet of war-proas floated lightly on the water, the black and yellow signal still fluttering from the flag ship. I could see now that the men that had come up the path behind me had brought a quantity of ropes. Perhaps there were thirty men in all. I wondered what they were going to do with me, but had decided that any fate was better than to be a Moro slave.

"Men of Mindanao," said the chief, "you know our errand. You know how often men of our band have been captured by the white men of the north to lie in prisons there, where death comes so slowly that a 'barong' blow would be paradise. The few that have crept back to us, weak, hollow-eyed and trembling, have only come to show us what it meant to starve, and then have died. The sky is just, and gives us once and again a white man to whom we may show that the prophet's words 'an eye for an eye and a tooth for a tooth,' are just. Give the white dog his due."

Two men grasped me and wound a stout rope, coil after coil, about me from my neck to my feet, until I was as helpless as a swathed Egyptian mummy. One end of another rope was fastened in a slip-noose about my body, and a dozen of the men, sitting well back from the edge of the cliff and bracing themselves one against an-other, paid out the rope.

The chief himself, touching me with his foot as he would have touched some unclean thing, rolled me over the brink of the precipice. The sharp rocks cut my face until the blood came, but that meant little to a man who expected to be dropped upon rocks just as sharp three hundred feet beneath him.

Slowly I was lowered down the face of the cliff until, perhaps twenty feet down, I found to my surprise that my descent had ceased, and that I was dangling before the mouth of a cave of considerable size. While I swung there, wondering what would happen next, the end of a rope ladder flung down from above dropped across the opening in the side of the cliff, and a moment later two agile Moros climbed down the ladder and from it entered the cave. From where they stood it was easy for them to reach out and haul me in after them, as a bale of merchandise swinging from a hoisting pulley is hauled in through a window.

Loosening the slip-knot they fastened into it the rope which had been coiled about my body, and giving it a jerk as a signal the whole was drawn up out of sight. Then, binding my feet again, they laid me on the hard rock near the mouth of the cave, and climbed nimbly back as they had come. The rope ladder was drawn up, and I was left alone.

I was to be left there to starve. That was what the chief's "eye for an eye and a tooth for a tooth" had meant.

From where they had left me I could see the proas at anchor, and see the rocky point on which we had landed. That night they built a fire on the rocks where I could see it; and feasted there with songs and dancing. Whenever the wind fresh-ened, the smell of the broiling fish came up to where I was, and I understood then why it was that I had not been fed that day as usual on the deck of the war-proa. I began to realise something of the depths of cruelty of the Moro nature. "Began," I say, for I found out later that even then I did not measure it all.

In the morning the proas were still at anchor, and during the day and night there was more feasting. Sometime that day I freed my hands. I found that the thongs had been nearly cut. Evidently the men who left me had meant that I should free myself. It was easy then to untie the rope which bound my ankles, but weak as I was from hunger, and cramped from being so long bound, it was some time before

I could bear my weight upon my feet. When I could it was the morning of the second day of my imprisonment and the third that I had been without food. The men below were sleeping after their carouse, stretched out on the decks of the proas. A sentinel on the rocky point poked the smouldering embers of the fire and raking out some overdone fragments of fish made a breakfast from them and pitched the bones into the sea. Only those who have lived three days without food can understand how delicious even those cast-off fish bones looked to me. I walked away from the mouth of the cave to be where I could not see the man eat. The daylight enabled me to explore the interior of the cave more thoroughly than I had been able to do before. From a crevice, far within, a tiny thread of water trickled down the rock. It was too thin to be called a stream, and was dried up entirely by the air before it reached the mouth of the cave, but I found that I could press my hand against the rock and after a long time gather water enough to moisten my lips and throat. For even that I was thankful. At least I should not die of thirst.

Still farther in the cave I found a pile of something lying on the floor. I could not see in the dark there what it was, but brought a double handful out to the light. It was a fragment of a military uniform wrapped loosely around some human bones. Dangling from the cloth was a corroded button on which I could still discern the insignia of Spain. I flung the horrid relics as far out from the cave as my weak strength would let me, and sank down, wondering how long it would be until the bones and uniform of a soldier of the United States would lie rotting there beside those of a soldier of Spain.

A shout from below aroused me. A Moro had seen the fragments of cloth fluttering down and had greeted them. The men had landed on the rocky point again, and a party of them were coming up the path. Slung on a pole carried over the shoulders of two of them was a piece of fish net, through the meshes of which I could see a dozen cocoanuts.

There was food; delicious food! And they were bringing it to me! I understood it all now. They had not meant to starve me, but only to torture me before they took me on to slavery. How good that was. Slavery did not seem hard to me now. Slavery was better than starvation. Oh I would work gladly enough, no matter how hard the task, if I could only have food.

The men had passed out of sight, now, climbing upward, and by and by I heard them talking above me. I leaned as far out from the mouth of the cave as in my weakness I dared, and looked up. Yes, I was right. The bag of cocoanuts was being lowered to me. I could see the black face of the Moro who was directing the operation, peering over the edge of the cliff. I sank down, too weak to stand. I thought I must save what little strength I had to break a nut against the rock, when they reached me.

I could see the bottom of the fish net bag. Now it was even with the cave. I could reach it if it was only a little nearer. Why did not those foolish Moros swing it nearer? I leaned out from the cave again to try and signal to them.

What was this I saw? Not one, but twenty black faces grinning down at me with devilish cruelty. And the bag of food that I had waited for, hung by a rope from the end of the pole pushed out from the rock above, swung lazily around and around just beyond my reach. I made a frantic effort to grasp it, and barely saved myself from falling headlong. The fiendish laughter of the men above was answered by a chorus of shouts from below. I looked down. From the decks of the proas and from about the fire on shore, where another feast was beginning, the Moro men were watching me.

Then I understood for the first time the depths of Moro cruelty. I was to be baited there until, crazed by hunger, I flung myself to an awful death upon the rocks below. I wondered how many men, perhaps braver soldiers than I, had gone down there before me.

I would not. If die I must, I would at least cheat those gibbering fiends of their show. I would die as that other man had done, far in the cave and out of sight. I dragged myself in, drank from the little stream of water, and lay down. I must have slept, or lain in a stupor for several hours, since, when I recovered myself again, it was late afternoon.

From where I lay I could see the bag of cocoanuts swing in the breeze. Perhaps it had blown nearer and I could reach it. I dragged myself out to the mouth of the cave again. It was just as far away as ever, and I too weak now to try to reach it. After a time I began to realise that there was no noise from the revelers below. I looked down. The bay was empty. The proas had gone, the men gone with them, and not a breath of smoke rising from the ashes showed where their fires had been. They must have put out their fires. Dimly I wondered why. Anyway I had cheated them of their game. They had become discouraged, waiting to see me die, and had gone.

These thoughts were passing weakly through my mind, when suddenly I saw something which made me stand up, weak as I was. Far out across the Strait of Mindoro a streamer of black smoke showed against the sky. My eyes followed it to where a gray hull rested on the water. It was one of our gunboats bound from Ilo Ilo back to Manila. I shouted, faintly, forgetting that miles of space lay between her and myself. I knew when I stopped to think that she was going from me. Even if she had come near Coron she had passed while I lay asleep.

That was why the proas had gone. They had seen the streak of smoke, and slipping behind the island of Coron had gone around Culion, and so on, home.

I must have slept for some time after that, for when I was next conscious of anything it was the forenoon of another day, and the cave was flooded with the bright light of noon. I did not suffer anything now. That seemed to have passed. I lay quite easy, and wondered what it was that had aroused me. After a while I could tell. It was the ceaseless twittering of a flock of birds which were flying in and out of the cave. They had not been there before, nor had I seen them about. They must have come during the night. I thought if I could catch one I would eat it, but I decided it was useless to try to catch them, they darted about so swiftly. By and by I felt sure that this was so, for I could see that the birds were swallows, and there came into my mind a vivid picture of the high beams of my father's barn, away in Vermont, when I was a boy, and the barn swallows flashing like arrows through the star-shaped openings far up in the gable ends.

Two of the birds had lighted on the wall opposite me, clinging to the rock. I wondered what they were doing there. Perhaps I could catch them. I would try. I found that I could rise, and that I was much stronger than I had thought. Even a hope of food seemed to give me strength. I crept towards the birds and put out my hand. The birds flew, and dodging me swept out into the sunlight. I was near enough the side of the cave now to see what they had been doing. Fastened to the rock was the beginning of what was to be a nest.

Once, years before that, I had been the guest of honor at a ten course Chinese dinner. After the tiny China cups of fiery liquor, which was the first course, had been drunk, the servant brought on what looked to me like fine white sponges boiled in chicken broth. My host told me that this was birds' nest soup, the most famous dish of China, made of material worth its weight in gold. It came back to me now that he had added that the best nests were gathered in the Philippine Islands. Little did I imagine then what that scrap of table conversation might one day mean to me.

I pulled the nest down and ate it. It looked like white glue, and tasted like beef jelly. I looked for another, and found it and ate it. There were no more. I drank my fill of water, when I could get it, which took some time, and then I lay down and went to sleep. I felt as if I had eaten a full meal. When I woke I could almost have danced, I felt so strong and well again. In my new strength I even tried to reach the bag of cocoanuts, but they hung just as far off as ever, and that was so far no breeze quite swung them within my reach. No matter! While I had slept, the birds had been at work, and half a dozen half-formed nests were glued to the rocks in easy reach. They grew like mushrooms in the night. I pulled down two and ate them. For dinner I had two more, and one for supper.

After that I had no cause to suffer, so far as food and water were concerned. When the birds built faster than my immediate wants required, I tore the completed nests down before the builders could spoil them, and stored them away. The birds twittered and scolded, but began to build again.

How long this would have lasted I do not know, but one morning when I woke and came to the mouth of the cave to look out, I saw that in the night a Chinese junk, with broad latteen sails, had dropped anchor in the bay below.

The shout of joy I gave came near being my ruin, for when the Chinese sailors heard it, and looked up to see a white faced figure gesticulating wildly in a hole in the front of the cliff, so far above them they thought, quite reasonably enough, that they had discovered the door to the home of the evil one himself, and that one of his ministers was trying to entice them to enter. Fortunately they could not flee until the anchor was raised and the sails unfurled, and before this was done their curiosity and common sense combined had conquered their fear. The leader of the expedition, I learned later, had been to Coron before, and now, lighting a few joss sticks as a precaution, in case I did prove to be an evil spirit, he climbed to the top of the cliff where he could talk with me. He had seen Moro fish nets and proa masts before, and he knew the Moro nature, so it did not take long to make him understand my story, nor much longer for him to effect my release, for these Chinese nest-hunting expeditions go fitted with all manner of rock scaling machinery in the way of rope ladders, slings and baskets.

I was very kindly treated on board the junk through all the month the party stayed there gathering nests, but when the men came to know my story, and learned how for two weeks I had lived on nothing but swallows' nests, worth their weight in gold, remember, they used to look at me, some of them, in a way which made me almost wonder if sometime when I was asleep they might not kill me, as the farmer's wife killed the goose that laid the golden egg.

THE CONJURE MAN OF SIARGAO

When I woke that morning, the monkey was sitting on the footboard of my bed, looking at me. Not one of those impudent beasts that do nothing but grin and chatter, but a solemn, old-man looking animal, with a fatherly, benevolent face.

All the same, monkeys are never to be trusted, even if you know more about them than I could about one which had appeared unannounced in my sleeping room over night.

"Filipe!" I shouted, "Filipe!"

The woven bamboo walls of a Philippine house allow sound and air to pass freely, and my native servant promptly entered the room.

"Take that monkey away," I said.

"Oh Senor," cried Filipe. "Never! You cannot mean it. The Conjure man of Siargao brought him to you this morning, as a gift. Much good always comes to the house which the Conjure man smiles on."

"Who in the name of Magellan is the Conjure man, and why is he smiling on me?" I asked.

"He is an old, old man who has lived back in the mountains for many years. He knows more conjure charms than any other man or woman in Siargao. The mountain apes come to his house to be fed, and people say that he can talk with them. He left no message, but brought the monkey, and said that the beast was for you."

"Well, take the creature out of the room while I dress, can't you?"

"Si, Senor," Filipe replied; but the way in which he went about the task showed that for him, at least, a gift monkey from the Conjure man of Siargao was no ordinary animal. The monkey, after gravely inspecting the hand which Filipe respectfully extended to him, condescended to step from the footboard of the bed upon it, and be borne from the room.

After that the "wise man," for I gave the little animal this name, was a regular member of my family, and in time I came to be attached to him. He was never mischievous or noisy, and would sit for an hour at a time on the back of a chair watching me while I wrote or read. He was expert in catching scorpions and the other nuisances of that kind which make Philippine housekeeping a burden to the flesh, and never after he was brought to me did we have any annoyance from them. He seemed to feel that the hunting of such vermin was his especial duty, and, in fact, I learned later that he had been regularly trained to do this.

Chiefly, though, he helped me in the increase of prestige which he gave me with the natives. Filipe treated me with almost as much respect as he did the monkey, when he realised that for some inscrutable reason the Conjure man had chosen to favour me with his friendship. The villagers, after that early morning visit, looked upon my thatched bamboo hut as a sort of temple, and I suspect more than once crept stealthily up conveniently close trees at night to try to peer between the slats of which the house was built, to learn in that way if they could, what the inner rooms of the temple were like.

My house was "up a tree." Up several trees, in fact. Like most of those in Siargao it was built on posts and the sawed off trunks of palm trees. The floor was eight feet above the ground, and we entered by way of a ladder which at night we drew up after us, or rather I drew up, for since Filipe slept at home, the "wise man" and I had our house to ourselves at night. The morning the monkey came, Filipe was prevailed upon to borrow a ladder from another house, and burglarise my home to the extent of putting the monkey in.

I had been in Siargao for two years, as the agent of a Hong Kong firm which was trying to build up the hemp industry there. That was before the American occupation of the islands. The village where I lived was the seaport. I would have been insufferably lonesome if I had not had something to interest me in my very abundant spare time, for during much of the year I was, or rather I had supposed I was, with the exception of the Padre, the only white man on the island. Twice a year the Spanish tax collector came and stayed long enough to wring every particle of money which he possibly could out of the poor natives, and then supplemented this by taking in addition such articles of produce as could be easily handled, and would have a money value in Manila.

The interest which I have referred to as sustaining me was in the plants, trees and flowers of the island. I was not a trained naturalist, but I had a fair knowledge of commercial tropic vegetation before I came to the island, and this had proved a good foundation to work on. Our hemp plantation was well inland, and in going to and from this I began to study the possibilities of the wild trees and plants. It ended in my being able to write a very fair description of the vegetation of this part of the archipelago, explaining how many of the plants might be utilized for medicine or food, and the trees for lumber, dyestuffs or food.

One who has not been there cannot begin to understand the possibilities of the forests under the hands of a man who really knows them. One of the first things which interested me was a bet Filipe made with me that he could serve me a whole meal, sufficient and palatable, and use nothing but bamboo in doing this.

The only thing Filipe asked to have to work with was a "machete," a sharp native sword. With this he walked to the nearest clump of bamboo, split open a dry joint, and cutting out two sticks of a certain peculiar shape made a fire by rubbing them together. Having got his fire he split another large green joint, the center of which he hollowed out. This he filled with water and set on the fire, where it would resist the action of the heat until the water in it boiled, just as I have seen water in a pitcher plant's leaf in America set on the coals of a blacksmith's fire and boiled vigorously. In this water he stewed some fresh young bamboo shoots, which make a most delicious kind of "greens," and finally made me from the wood a platter off which to eat and a knife and fork to eat with. I acknowledged that he had won the bet.

It was on one of the excursions which I made into the forest in my study of these natural resources, that I met the Conjure man. I had been curious to see him ever since he had called on me that morning before I was awake, and left the "wise man," in lieu of a card, but inquiry of Filipe and various other natives invariably elicited the reply that they did not know where he lived. I learned afterwards that the liars went to him frequently, for charms and medicines to use in sickness, at the very time they were telling me that they did not even know in what part of the forest his home was. Later events showed that fear could make them do what coaxing could not.

It happened that one of my expeditions took me well up the side of a mountain which the natives called Tuylpit, so near as I could catch their pronunciation. I never saw the name in print. The mountain's sides were rocky enough so that they were not so impassable on account of the dense under-growth as much of the island was, and I had much less trouble than usual going forward after I left the regular "carabaos" (water buffalo) track.

I had gone on up the mountain for some distance, Filipe, as usual, following me, when, turning to speak to him, I found to my amazement that the fellow was gone. How, when or where he had disappeared I could not imagine, for he had answered a question of mine only a moment before.

If I had been surprised to find myself alone, I was ten times more surprised to turn back again and find that I was not alone.

A man stood in the path in front of me, an old man, but standing well erect, and with keen dark eyes looking out at me from under shaggy white eyebrows.

I knew at once, or felt rather than knew, for the knowledge was instinctive, that this must be the Conjure man of Siargao, but I was dumbfounded to find him, not, as I had supposed, a native, but a white man, as surely as I am one. Before I could pull myself together enough to speak to him, he spoke to me, in Spanish, calling me by name.

"You see I know your name," he said, and then added, as if he saw the question in my eyes, "Yes, it was I who brought the monkey to your house. I knew so long as he was there no man or woman on this island would molest you.

"You wonder why I did it? Because in all the time you have been here, and in all your going about the island, you have never cruelly killed the animals, as most white men do who come here. The creatures of the forest are all I have had to love, for many years, and I have liked you because you have spared them. How I happened to come here first, and why I have stayed here all these years, is nothing to you. Quite likely you would not be so comfortable here alone with me if you knew. Anyway, you are not to know. You are alone, you see. Your servant took good care to get out of the way when he knew that I was coming."

"How did you know my name," I made out to ask, "and so much about me?"

"The natives have told me much of you, when they have been to me for medicines, which they are too thickheaded to see for themselves, although they grow beneath their feet. Then I have seen you many times myself, when you have been in the forest, and had no idea that I, or any one, for that matter, was watching you."

"Why do I see you now, then?" I asked.

"Because the desire to speak once more to a white man grew too strong to be resisted. Because you happened to come, to-day, near my home, to which," he added, with a very courteous inclination of his head, "I hope that you will be so good as to accompany me."

I wish that I could describe that strange home so that others could see it as I did.

Imagine a big, broad house, thatched, and built of bamboo, like all of those in Siargao, that the earthquakes need not shake them down, but built, in this case, upon the ground. A man to whom even the snakes of the forest were submissive, as they were to this man, had no need to perch in trees, as the rest of us must do, in order to sleep in safety. Above the house the plumy tops of a group of great palm trees waved in the air. Birds, more beautiful than any I had ever seen on the island, flirted their brilliant feathers in the trees around the house, and in the vines which laced the tops of the palm trees together a troop of monkeys was chattering. The birds showed no fear of us, and one, a gorgeous paroquet, flew from the tree in which it had been perched and settled on the shoulder of the Conjure man. The monkeys, when they saw us, set up a chorus of welcoming cries, and began letting themselves down from the tree tops. My guide threw a handful of rice on the ground for the bird, and tossed a basket of tamarinds to where the monkeys could get them. Then, having placed me in a comfortable hammock woven of cocoanut fibre, and brought me a pipe and some excellent native tobacco, he slung another hammock for himself, and settled down in it to ask me questions.

Imagine telling the news of the world for the last quarter of a century to an intelligent and once well-educated man who has known nothing of what has happened in all that time except what he might learn from ignorant natives, who had obtained their knowledge second hand from Spanish tax collectors only a trifle less ignorant than themselves.

Just in the middle of a sentence I became aware that some one was looking at me from the door of the house behind me. Somebody or something, I had an uncomfortable feeling that I did not quite know which. I twisted around in the hammock to where I could look.

An enormous big ape stood erect in the doorway, steadying herself by one hand placed against the door casing. She was looking at me intently, as if she did not just know what to do.

My host had seen me turn in the hammock. "Europa," he said, and then added some words which I did not understand.

The huge beast came towards me, walking erect, and gravely held out a long and bony paw for me to shake. Then, as if satisfied that she had done all that hospitality demanded of her, she walked to the further end of the thatch verandah and stood there looking off into the forest, from which there came a few minutes later the most unearthly and yet most human cry I ever heard.

I sprang out of my hammock, but before I could ask, "what was that?" the big ape had answered the cry with another one as weird as the first.

"Sit down, I beg of you," my host said. "That was only Atlas, Europa's mate, calling to her to let us know that he is nearly home. They startled you. I should have introduced them to you before now."

While he was still talking, another ape, bigger than the first, came in sight beneath the palms. Europa went to meet him, and they came to the house together.

As I am a living man that enormous animal, uncanny looking creature, walked up to me and shook hands. The Conjure man had not spoken to him, that was certain. If any one had told him to do this it must have been Europa. The demands of politeness satisfied, the strange couple went to the farther side of the verandah and squatted down in the shade.

"Can you talk with them?" I suddenly made bold to ask.

"Who told you I could?" the Conjure man inquired sharply.

"Filipe," I said.

But his question was the only answer my question ever received.

Later, when I said it was time for me to start for home, he set me out a meal of fruit and boiled rice. I quite expected to hear him order Europa to wait on the table, but he did not, and when I came away, and he came with me down the mountain as far as the "carabaos" track, the two big apes stayed on the verandah as if to guard the house.

When we parted at the foot of the mountain, although I am sure he had enjoyed my visit, my strange host did not ask me to come again, and when he gently declined my invitation for him to come and see me, I did not repeat it. I had a feeling that it would do no good to urge him, and that if a time ever came when he wanted to see me again he would make the wish known to me of his own accord.

It was not more than a month after my visit to the mountain home that the Spanish tax collector came for his semi-annual harvest. The boat which brought him would call for him a month later, and in the intervening time he would have got together all the property which could be squeezed or beaten out of the miserable natives. This particular man had been there before, and I heartily disliked him, as the worst of his kind I had yet seen. Inasmuch as he represented the government to which I also had to pay taxes and was, except for the Padre, about the only white man I saw unless it was when some of our own agents came to Siargao, I felt disgusted when I saw that this man had returned. He brought with him, on this trip, as a servant, a good-for-nothing native who had gone away with him six months before to save his neck from the just wrath of his own people for a crime which he had committed. Secure in the protection afforded by his employer's position, and the squad of Tagalog soldiers sent to help in collecting the taxes, this man had the effrontery to come back and swell about among his fellow people, any one of whom would have cut his throat in a minute if they could have done it without fear of detection by the tax collector.

I noticed, though, that the servant was particularly careful to sleep in the same house with his master, and did not go home at night, as Filipe did. The government representative had a house of his own, which was occupied only when he was on the island. It was somewhat larger than the other houses of the place, but like them was built on posts well up from the ground, and reached by a ladder which could be taken up at will, as, I noticed, it always was at night.

When the collector had been in Siargao less than a week, I was surprised to have him come to my place one day and ask me abruptly if I had ever seen any big apes in my excursions over the island.

I am obliged to confess that I lied to him very promptly and directly, for I told him at once that I never had. You see there had come into my mind at once what the lonely old man on the mountain had said about men who came and killed the animals he loved, and I could see as plainly as when I left them there, the two big apes sitting on the verandah of his home, watching us as we came down the mountain path, and waiting to welcome him when he came home.

The "wise man," sitting on top of the tallest piece of furniture in the room, to which he had promptly mounted when my caller came in, said nothing, but his solemn eyes looked at me in a way which makes me half willing to swear that he had understood every word, and countenanced my untruthfulness.

The tax collector looked up at the monkey suspiciously, as if he sometime might have heard how the animal came into my possession, as, in fact, I had reason afterwards to think he had.

"Caramba," he grunted. "I have reason to think there are big apes here. Juan," his black-leg--in every sense of the word--servant, "has told me there is an old man here who has tamed them. He says he knows where the man lives, back in the mountains.

"If I can find a big ape while I am here, this time," he went on, "I mean to have him or his hide. There was an agent for a museum of some kind in England, in Manila when I came away, and he told me he would give me fifty dollars for the skin of such a beast."

He went on talking in this way for quite a while, but I did not more than half hear what he was saying, for I was trying to think of some way in which I could send word to the old man to guard his companions. I finally decided, however, that Juan, though quite vile enough to do such a thing, would never dare to guide his employer to the Conjure man's house.

I did not properly measure the heart of a native doubly driven by hate of a former master from whom he is free, and fear of a master by whom he is employed at the present time.

The very next day Juan went to the Conjure man's house, and in his master's name demanded that one of the apes be brought, dead or alive, to the tax collector's office.

The only answer he brought back, except a slashed face on which the blood was even then not dry, was:

"Does a father slay his children at a stranger's bidding?"

The next day I was in the forest all day long. When I came home in the edge of the evening, and passed the tax collector's house, I said words which I should not wish to write down here, although I almost believe that the tears which were running down my cheeks at the time washed the record of my language off the recording angel's book, just as they would have blotted out the words upon this sheet of paper.

Europa, noble great animal, lay dead on the ground in front of the house, the slim, strong paw, like a right hand, which she had reached out to welcome me, drabbled with dirt where it had dragged behind the "carabaos" cart in which she had been brought, and which had been hardly large enough to hold her huge body.

I knew it was Europa. I would have known her anywhere, even if Filipe, white with fear and rage, had not told me the story when I reached home.

Juan had guided the tax collector to the mountain home in an evil moment when its owner and Atlas, by some chance were away. The Spaniard had shot Europa, standing in the door, as I had seen her standing, and the two men had brought the body down the mountain.

I think Filipe, and perhaps the other natives, expected nothing less than that the village, if not the whole island, would be destroyed by fire from the sky, that night, or swallowed up in the earth, but the night passed with perfect quiet. Not a sound was heard, nor a thing done to disturb our sleep, or if, as I imagine was the case with some of us who did not sleep, our peace.

Only, in the morning, when no one was seen stirring about the tax collector's house, and then it grew noon and the lattices were not opened or the ladder let down, the Tagalog soldiers brought another ladder and put it against the house, and I climbed up and went in, to find the two men who stayed there, the Spaniard and Juan, dead on the floor. Their swollen faces, black and awful to look at, I have seen in bad dreams since. On the throat of each were the blue marks of long, strong fingers.

And the body of Europa was gone.

MRS. HANNAH SMITH, NURSE

The red eye of the lighthouse on Corregidor Island blazed out through the darkness as a Pacific steamer felt her way cautiously into Manila harbour. Although it was nearly midnight, a woman--one of the passengers on the steamer--was still on deck, and standing well up toward the bow of the boat was peering into the darkness before her as if she could not wait to see the strange new land to which she was coming. Surely it would be a strange land to her, who, until a few weeks before had scarcely in all her life been outside of the New England town in which she had been born.

People who had seen her on the steamer had wondered sometimes that a woman of her age--for she was not young--should have chosen to go to the Philippine Islands as a nurse, as she told them she was going. Sometimes, at first, they smiled at some of her questions, but any who happened to be ill on the voyage, or in trouble, forgot to do that, for in the touch of her hand and in her words there was shown a skill and a nobleness of nature which won respect.

The colonel of a regiment stationed near Manila was sitting in his headquarters. An orderly came to the door and saluted.

"A woman to see you, sir," he said.

"A woman? What kind of a woman?"

"A white woman, sir. Looks about fifty years old. Talks American. Says she has only just come here. Says her name is Smith."

"Show her in."

The man went out. In a few minutes he came back again, and with him the woman that had stayed out on the deck of the Pacific steamer when the boat came past the light of Corregidor.

The Colonel gave his visitor a seat. "What can I do for you?" he said.

"Can I speak to you alone?"

"We are alone now."

"Can't that man out there hear?" motioning toward a soldier pacing back and forth before the door.

"No," said the officer. "We are quite alone."

The woman unfolded a sheet of paper which she had been holding, and looked at it a moment. Then she looked at the officer. "I want to see Heber Smith, of Company F, of your regiment," she said. "Can you tell me where he is?"

In spite of himself--in spite of the self possession which he would have said his campaigning experience had given him, the Colonel started.

"Are you his--?" he began to say. But he changed the question to, "Was he a relative of yours?"

"I am his mother," the woman said, as if she had completed the officer's first question in her mind and answered it.

"I have a letter from him, here," she went on. "The last one I have had. It is dated three months ago. It is not very long." She held up a half sheet of paper, written over on one side with a lead pencil; but she did not offer to let the officer read what was written.

"He tells me in this letter," the woman said, "that he has disgraced himself, been a coward, run away from some danger which he ought to have faced; and that he can't stand the shame of it." "He says," the woman's voice faltered for the first time, and instead of looking the Colonel in the face, as she had been doing, her eyes were fixed on the floor--"he says that he isn't going to try to stay here any longer, and that he is going over to the enemy. Is this true? Did he do that?"

"Yes," said the officer slowly. "It is true."

"He says here," the woman went on, holding up the letter again, "that I shall never hear from him again, or see him. I want you to help me to find him."

"I would be glad to help you if I could," the man said, "but I cannot. No one knows where the man went to, except that he disappeared from the camp and from the city. Besides I have not the right. He was a coward, and now he is a deserter. If he came back now he would have to stand trial, and he might be shot."

"He is not a coward." The woman's cheeks flamed red. "Some men shut their eyes and cringe when there comes a flash of lightning. But that don't make them cowards. He might have been frightened at the time, and not known what he was doing, but he is not a coward. I guess I know that as well as anybody can tell me. He is my boy--my only child. I've come out here to find him, and I'm going to do it. I don't expect I'll find him quick or easy, perhaps. I've let out our farm for a year, with the privilege of renewing the trade when the year is up; and I'm going to stay as long as need be. I'm not going to sit still and hold my hands while I'm waiting, either. I'm going to be a nurse. I know how to take care of the sick and maimed all right, and I guess from what I hear since I've been here you need all the help of that kind you can get. All I want of you is to get me a chance to work nursing just as close to the front as I can go, and then do all you can to help me find out where Heber is, and then let me have as many as you can of these heathen prisoners the men bring in here to take care of, so I can ask them if they have seen Heber. My boy isn't a coward, and if he has got scared and run away, he's got to come back and face the music. Thank goodness none of the folks at home know anything about it, and they won't if I can help it."

The woman folded the letter, and putting it back into its envelope sat waiting. It was evident that she did not conceive of the possibility even of her request not being granted.

The officer hesitated.

"You will have to see the General, Mrs. Smith," he said at last, glad that it need not be his duty to tell her how hopeless her errand was. "I will arrange for you to see him. I will take you to him myself. I wish I could do more to help you."

"How soon can I see him?"

"Tomorrow, I think. I will find out and let you know."

"Thank you," said the woman, as she rose to go. "I don't want to lose any time. I want to get right to work."

The next day the young soldier's mother saw the General and told her story to him. In the mean time, apprised by the Colonel of the regiment of the woman's errand, the General had had a report of the case brought to him. Heber Smith had been sent out with a small scouting party. They had been ambushed, and instead of trying to fight, he had left the men and had run back to cover.

"But that don't necessarily make him a coward," the young man's mother pleaded with the General. "A coward is a man who plans to run away. He lost his head that time. Wasn't that the first time he had been put in such a place?"

The officer admitted that it was.

"Well, then he can live it down. He has got to, for the sake of his father's reputation as well as his own. His father was a soldier, too," she said proudly. "He was in the Union army four years, and had a medal given to him for bravery, and every spring since he died the members of his Grand Army Post have decorated his grave. When Heber comes to think of that, I know he will come back."

The General was not an old man;--that is he was not so old but that, back in her prairie home in a western state, there was a mother to whom he wrote letters, a mother whom he knew to value above his life itself his reputation. The thought of her came to him now.

"I will do what I can, Mrs. Smith" he said, "to help you find your boy. I fear I cannot give you any hope, though, and if he should be found I cannot promise you anything as to his future."

"Thank you," said the woman. "That is all I can ask."

And so it came about that Mrs. Hannah Smith was enrolled as a nurse, and assigned to duty as near the front in the island of Luzon as any nurse could go.

Six months passed, and then another six came near to their end. Mrs. Smith renewed the lease of the farm back among the New England hills for another year, and wrote to a neighbor's wife to see that her woolen clothes and furs were aired and then packed away with a fresh supply of camphor to keep the moths out of them.

In this year's time Mrs. Smith had picked up a wonderful smattering of the Spanish and Tagalog languages for a woman who had lived the life she had before she came to the East. The reason for this, so her companions said, was her being "just possessed to talk with those native prisoners who are brought wounded to the hospital." The other nurses liked her. She not only was willing to take the cases they liked least--the natives--but asked for them.

And sometime in the course of their hospital experience, all Mrs. Smith's native patients--if they did not die before they got able to talk coherently--had to go through the same catechism:

Was there a white man among the people from whom they had come; a white man who had come there from the American army?

Was he a tall young man with light hair and a smooth face?

Did he have a three-cornered white scar on one side of his chin, where a steer had hooked him when he was a boy?

Did he look like this picture? (A photograph was shown the patient)

From no one, though, did she get the answer that her heart craved. Some of the prisoners knew white men that had come among the Tagalog natives, but no one knew a man who answered to this description.

One day a native prisoner who had been brought in more than a week before, terribly wounded, opened his eyes to consciousness for the first time, after days and nights of stupor. He was one of these who naturally fell, now, to "Mrs. Smith's lot," as the surgeons called them. As soon as the nurse's watchful eyes saw the change in the man she came to him and bent over his cot.

"Water, please," he murmured

The woman brought the water, her two natures struggling to decide what she should do after she had given it to him. As nurse, she knew the man ought not to be allowed to talk then. As mother, she was impatient to ask him where he had learned to speak English, and to inquire if he knew her boy.

The nurse conquered. The patient drank the water and was allowed to go to sleep again undisturbed.

In time, though, he was stronger, and then, one day, the mother's questions were asked for the hundredth time; and the last.

Yes, the prisoner patient knew just such a man. He had come among the people of the tribe many months ago. He was a tall, fair young man, and he had such a scar as the "senora," described. He was a fine young man. Once, when this man's father had been sick, the white man had doctored him and made him well. It was this white man, the patient said, who had taught him the little English that he knew.

"Yes," when he saw the photograph of Heber Smith, "that is the man. He has a picture, too," the patient said, "two pictures, little ones, set in a little gold box which hangs on his watch chain."

The hospital nurse unclasped a big cameo breast pin from the throat of her gown and held it down so that the man in bed could see a daguerreotype set in the back of the pin.

"Was one of the pictures like that?" she asked.

The Tagalog looked at the picture, a likeness of a middle-aged man wearing the coat and hat of the Grand Army of the Republic. In the picture a medal pinned on to the breast of the man's coat showed.

"Yes," said he, "one of the pictures is like that."

Then he looked up curiously at the woman sitting beside his bed. "The other picture is that of a woman," he went on, "and--yes--" still studying her face, "I think it must be you. Only," he added, "it doesn't look very much like you."

"No," said the woman, with a grim smile, "it doesn't. It was taken a good many years ago, when I was younger than I am now, and when I hadn't been baked for a year in this heathen climate. It's me, though."

In time, Juan, that was the man's name, was so far recovered of his wound that he was to be discharged from the hospital and placed with the other able-bodied prisoners. The hospital at that time occupied an old convent. The day before Juan was to be discharged, Mrs. Smith managed her cases so that for a time no one else was left in one of the rooms with her but this man.

"Juan," she said, when she was sure they were alone, and that no one was any-where within hearing, "do you feel that I have done anything to help you to get well?"

The man reached down, and taking one of the nurse's hands in his own bent over and kissed it.

"Senora," he said, "I owe my life to you."

"Will you do something for me, then? Something which I want done more than anything else in the world?"

"My life is the senora's. I would that I had ten lives to give her."

The woman pulled a letter from out the folds of her nurse's dress. The envelope was not sealed, and before she fastened it she took the letter which was in it out and read it over for one last time. Then, pulling from her waist a little red, white and blue badge pin--one of those patriotic emblems which so many people wear at times--she dropped this into the letter, sealed the envelope, and handed it to the Tagalog. The envelope bore no address.

"I hav'n't put the name of the place on it you said you came from," she told the man, "because goodness only knows how it is spelled; I don't. Besides that, it isn't necessary. You know the place, and you know the man; the man who has got my picture and his father's in a gold locket on his watch chain. I want you to give this letter into his own hands. I expect it will be rather a ticklish job for you to get away from here and get through the lines, but I guess you can do it if you try. Other men have. Don't start until you are well enough so you will have strength to make the whole trip."

A week or so after that, one of the surgeons making his daily visit reported that Juan had made his escape the previous night, and up to that time had not been brought back.

"What a shame!" said one of the other nurses. "After all the care you gave that man, Mrs. Smith. It does seem as if he might have had a little more gratitude."

Mrs. Smith said nothing aloud. But to herself, when she was alone, she said: "Well, I suppose some folks would say that I wasn't acting right, but I guess I've saved the lives of enough of those men since I've been here so that I'm entitled to one of them if I want him."

Then she went on with her work, and waited; and the waiting was harder than the work.

An American expedition was slowly toiling across the island of Luzon to locate and occupy a post in the north. Four companies of men marched in advance, with a guard in the rear. Between them were the mule teams with the camp luggage and the ever present hospital corps. No trace of the enemy had been seen in that part of the island for weeks. Scouts who had gone on in advance had reported the way to be clear, and the force was being hurried up to get through a ravine which it was approaching, so it could go into camp for the night on high, level ground just beyond the valley.

Suddenly a man's voice rang out upon the hot air; an English, speaking voice, strong and clear, and coming, so it seemed at first to the troops when they heard it, from the air above them:

"Halt! Halt!" the voice cried.

"Go back! There is an ambush on both sides! Save yourselves! Be--"

The warning was unfinished. Those of the Americans who had located the sound of the words and had looked in the direction from which they came, had seen a white man standing on the rocky side of the ravine above them and in front of them. They had seen him throw up his arms and fall backward out of sight, leaving his last sentence unfinished. Then there had come the report of a gun, and then an attack, with scores of shouting Tagalogs swarming down the sides of the ravine.

The skirmish was over, though, almost as soon as it had begun, and with little harm to any of the Americans except to such of the scouts as had been cut off in advance. The warning had come in time--had come before the advancing column had marched between the forces hidden on both sides of the ravine. The Tagalogs could not face the fire with which the Americans met them. They fled up the ravine, and up both sides of the gorge, into the shelter of the forest, and were gone. The Americans, satisfied at length that the way was clear, moved forward and went into camp on the ground which had previously been chosen, throwing out advance lines of pickets, and taking extra precautions to be prepared against a night attack.

Early in the evening shots were heard on the outer picket line, and a little later two men came to the commanding officers tent bringing with them a native.

"He was trying to come through our lines and get into the camp, sir," they reported. "Two men fired at him, but missed him."

"Think he's a spy?" the commander asked of another officer who was with him.

"No, Senor, I am not a spy," the prisoner said, surprising all the men by speaking in English. "I have left my people, I want to be sent to Manila, to the American camp there."

"He's a deserter," said one of the officers. Then to the men who held the prisoner, "Better search him."

From out the prisoner's blouse one of the soldiers brought a paper, a sheet torn from a note book, folded, and fastened only by a red, white and blue badge pin stuck through the paper.

The officer to whom the soldier had handed the paper pulled out the pin which had kept it folded, and started to open it, when he saw there was something written on the side through which the pin had been thrust. Bending down to where the camp light fell upon the writing, he saw that it was an address, scrawled in lead pencil:

"Mrs. Hannah Smith; Nurse."

"Do you know the woman to whom this letter is sent? he asked in amazement of the Tagalog from whom it had been taken.

"Yes Senor."

"Do you know where she is now?"

"Yes, Senor. She is in a hospital not far from Manila. She is a good woman. My life is hers. I was there once for many, many days, shot through here," he placed his hand on his side, "and she made me well again."

"Do you know who sent this letter to her?"

"Yes, Senor."

"Who was it?"

The man hesitated.

"Who was it? Answer. It is for her good I want to know."

"It was her son, Senor."

"Was he the man who gave us warning of the ambush today?"

"Yes, Senor."

The officer folded the paper, unread, and thrust the pin back through the folds. The enamel on the badge glistened in the camp light.

"Keep the Tagalog here," he said to the men, "until I come back;" and walked across the camp to where the hospital tents had been set up.

"Where is Mrs. Smith?" he asked of the surgeon in charge.

"Taking care of the men who were wounded this afternoon."

"Will you tell her that I want to see her alone in your tent, here, and then see that no one else comes in?"

"Mrs. Smith," he said, when the nurse came in, "I have something here for you--a letter. It has just been brought into camp, by a native who did not know that you were here and who wanted to be sent to Manila to find you. It is not very strongly sealed, but no one has read it since it was brought into camp."

He gave the bit of paper to the nurse, and then turned away to stand in the door of the tent, that he might not look at her while she read it. Enough of the nurse's story was known in the army now so that the officer could guess something of what this message might mean to her.

A sound in the tent behind the officer made him turn. The woman had sunk down on the ground beneath the surgeon's light, and resting her arms upon a camp stool had hid her face.

A moment later she raised her head, her face wet with tears and wearing an expression of mingled grief and joy, and held out the letter to the officer.

"Read it!" she said. "Thank God!" and then, "My boy! My boy!" and hid her face again.

"Dear mother," the scrawled note read.

"I got your letter. I'm glad you wrote it. It made things plain I hadn't seen before. My chance has come--quicker than I had expected. I wish I might have seen you again, but I shan't. A column of our men are coming up the valley just below here, marching straight into an ambush. I have tried to get word to them, but I can't, because the Tagalogs watch me so close. They never have trusted me. The only way for me is to rush out when the men get near enough, and shout to them, and that will be the end of it all for me. I don't care, only that I wish I could see you again. Juan will take this letter to you. When you get it, and the men come back, if I save them, I think perhaps they will clear my name. Then you can go home.

"The men are almost here. Mother, dear, good by.--Your Boy."

"I wish I might have seen him," the woman said, a little later. "But I won't complain. What I most prayed God for has been granted me."

"They'll let the charge against him drop, now, won't they? Don't you think he has earned it?"

"I think he surely has. No braver deed has been done in all this war."

"Don't try to come, now, Mrs Smith," as the nurse rose to her feet. "Stay here, and I will send one of the women to you."

When he had done this the officer went back to where the men were still holding Juan between them.

"Your journey is shorter than you thought," the officer said to the Tagalog. "Mrs. Smith is in this camp, and I have given the letter to her."

"May I see her?" exclaimed the man.

"Not now. In the morning you may. Have you seen this man, her son, since he was shot?"

"No, Senor. He gave me the note and told me to slip into the forest as soon as the fight began, so as to get away without any one seeing me. Then I was to stay out of the way until I could get into this camp."

"Do you know where he stood when he was shot?"

"Yes, Senor."

"Can you take a party of men there tonight?"

"Yes, Senor; most gladly."

Afterward, when it came to be known that Heber Smith would live, in spite of his wounds and the hours that he had lain there in the bushes unconscious and uncared for, there was the greatest diversity of opinion as to what had really saved his life.

The surgeons said it was partly their skill, and partly the superb constitution that years of work on a New England farm had given to the young man. His mother believed that he had been spared for her sake. Heber Smith himself always said it was his mother's care that saved his life, while Juan never had the least doubt that the young soldier had been protected solely by a marvellous "anting-anting" which he himself had slipped unsuspected into the American soldier's blouse that day, before he had left him. As soon as she knew that her son would live, Mrs. Smith started for Washington, carrying with her papers which made it possible for her to be allowed to plead her case there as she had pleaded it in Manila. A pardon was sent back, as fast as wire and steamer and wire again could convey it. Heber Smith wears the uniform of a second lieutenant, now, won for bravery in action since he went back into the service; and every one who knew her in the Philippines, cherishes the memory of Mrs. Hannah Smith; Nurse.

THE FIFTEENTH WIFE

Mateo, my Filipino servant, was helping me sort over specimens one day under the thatched roof of a shed which I had hired to use for such work while I was on the island of Culion, when I was startled to see him suddenly drop the bird skin he had been working on, and fall upon his knees, bending his body forward, his face turned toward the road, until his forehead touched the floor.

At first I thought he must be having some new kind of a fit, peculiar to the Philippine Islands, until I happened to glance up the road toward the town, from which my house was a little distance removed, and saw coming toward us a most remarkable procession.

Four native soldiers walked in front, two carrying long spears, and two carrying antiquated seven-foot muskets, relics of a former era in fire arms. After the soldiers came four Visayan slaves, bearing on their shoulders a sort of platform covered with rugs and cushions, on which a woman reclined. On one side of the litter walked another slave, holding a huge umbrella so as to keep the sun's rays off the woman's face. Two more soldiers walked behind.

Mateo might have been a statue, or a dead man, for all the attention he paid to my questions until after the procession had passed the house. Then, resuming a perpendicular position once more, he said, "That was the Sultana Ahmeya, the Sultana."

Then he went on to explain that there were thirteen other sultanas, of assorted colors, who helped make home happy for the Sultan of Culion, who after all, well supplied as he might at first seem to be, was only a sort of fourth-class sovereign, so far as sultanas are concerned, since his fellow monarch on a neighboring larger island, the Sultan of Sulu, is said to have four hundred wives.

Ahmeya, though, Mateo went on to inform me, was the only one of the fourteen who really counted. She was neither the oldest nor the youngest of the wives of the reigning ruler, but she had developed a mind of her own which had made her supreme in the palace, and besides, she was the only one of his wives who had borne a son to the monarch. For her own talents, and as the mother of the heir, the people did her willing homage.

When I saw the royal cavalcade go past my door I had no idea I would ever have a chance to become more intimately acquainted with Her Majesty, but only a little while after that circumstances made it possible for me to see more of the royal family than had probably been the privilege of any other white man. How little thought I had, when the acquaintance began, of the strange experiences it would eventually lead to!

At that time, in the course of collecting natural history specimens, most of my time for three years was spent in the island of Culion. Having a large stock of drugs, for use in my work, and quite a lot of medicines, I had doctored Mateo and two or three other fellows who had worked for me, when they had been ill, with the result that I found I had come to have a reputation for medical skill which sometimes was inconvenient. I had no idea how widely my fame had spread, though, until one morning Mateo came into my room and woke me, and with a face which expressed a good deal of anxiety, informed me that I was sent for to come to the palace.

I confess I felt some concern myself, and should have felt more if I had had as much experience then as I had later, for one never knows what those three-quarters savage potentates may take it into their heads to do.

When I found that I was sent for because the Sultan was ill,--ill unto death, the messenger had made Mateo believe,--and I was expected to doctor him, I did not feel much more comfortable, for I much doubted if my knowledge of diseases, and my assortment of medicines, were equal to coping with a serious case. If the Sultan died I would probably be beheaded, either for not keeping him alive, or for killing him.

It was a great relief, then, when I reached the palace, and just before I entered the room where the sick monarch was, to hear him swearing vigorously, in a combination of the native and Spanish languages which was as picturesque as it was expressive.

I found the man suffering from an acute attack of neuralgia, although he did not know what was the matter with him. He had not been able to sleep for three days and nights, and the pain, all the way up and down one side of his face had been so intense that he thought he was going to die, and almost hoped that he was. His head was tied up in a lot of cloths, not over clean, in which a dozen native doctor's charms had been folded, until the bundle was as big as four heads ought to be.

As soon as I found out what was the matter I felt relieved, for I reckoned I could manage an attack of swelled head all right. I had doctored the natives enough, already, to find out that they had no respect for remedies which they could not feel, and so, going back to the house, I brought from there some extra strong liniment, some tincture of red pepper and a few powerful morphine pills.

I gave my patient one of the pills the first thing, administering it in a glass of water with enough of the cayenne added to it so that the mixture brought tears to his eyes, and then removing the layers of cloth from his head, and gathering in as I did so, for my collection of curiosities, the various charms which I uncovered, I gave his head a vigorous shampooing with the liniment, taking pains to see that the liquor occasionally ran down into the Sultan's eyes. He squirmed a good deal, but I kept on until I thought it must be about time for the morphine to begin to take effect. I kept him on morphine and red pepper for three days, but when I let up on him he was cured, and my reputation was made.

It would have been too great a nuisance to have been endured, had it not been that so high a degree of royal favor enabled me to pursue my work with a degree of success which otherwise I could never have hoped for.

After that I used to see a good deal of the palace life. Although nominally Mohammedans in religion, the inhabitants of these more distant islands have little more than the name of the faith, and follow out few of its injunctions. As a result I was accorded a freedom about the palace which would have been impossible in such an establishment in almost any other country.

One day the Sultan had invited me to dine with him. After the meal, while we were smoking, reclining in some cocoanut fibre hammocks swung in the shade of the palace court yard, I saw a man servant lead a dog through the square, and down a narrow passage way through the rear of the palace.

"Would you like to see the 'Green Devil' eat?" my host asked.

I have translated the native words he used by the term "green devil," because that represents the idea of the original better than any other words I know of, I had not the slightest conception as to who or what the individual referred to might be; but I said at once that I would be very glad indeed to see him eat.

My host swung out of the hammock,--he was a superbly strong and vigorous man, now that he was in health again,--and led the way through the passage. Following him I found myself in another court yard, larger than the first, and with more trees in it. Beneath one of these trees, in a stout cage of bamboo, was the biggest python I ever saw. He must have been fully twenty-five feet long. The cage was large enough to give the snake a chance to move about in it, and when we came in sight he was rolling from one end to the other with head erect, eyes glistening, and the light shimmering on his glossy scales in a way which made it easy to see why he had been given his name. I learned later that he had not been fed for a month, and that he would not be fed again until another month had passed. Like all of his kind he would touch none but live food.

The wretched dog, who seemed to guess the fate in store for him, hung back in the rope tied about his neck, and crouched flat to the ground, too frightened even to whine.

The servant unlocked a door in the side of the cage and thrust the poor beast in. I am not ashamed to say that I turned my head away. It was only a dog, but it might have been a human being, so far as the reptile, or the half-savage man at my side, would have cared.

When I looked again, the dog was only a crushed mass of bones and flesh, about which the snake was still winding and tightening coil after coil.

"We need not wait," the Sultan said. "It will be an hour before he will swallow the food. You can come out again."

I did as he suggested. It was a wonder to me, as it is to every one, how a snake's throat can be distended enough to swallow whole an object so large as this dog, but in some way the reptile had accomplished the feat. The meal over, the huge creature had coiled down as still almost as if dead. He would lie in that way, now, they told me, for days.

It was while I stood watching the snake that Ahmeya came through the square, leading her boy by the hand. The apartments of the royal wives were built around this inner yard. This was the first time I had seen the heir to the throne. He was a handsome boy, and looked like his mother. Ahmeya was tall, for a native woman, and carried herself with a dignity which showed that she felt the honor of her position. Mateo had told me that she had a decided will of her own, and, so the palace gossips said, ruled the establishment, and her associate sultanas, with an unbending hand.

It was not very long after I had seen the green devil eat that Mateo told me there had been another wedding at the palace. Mateo was an indefatigable news-gatherer, and an incorrigible gossip. As the society papers would have expressed it, this wedding had been "a very quiet affair." The Sultan had happened to see a Visayan girl of uncommon beauty, on one of the smaller islands, one day, had bought her of her father for two water buffalos, and had installed her at the palace as wife number fifteen.

For the time being the new-comer was said to be the royal favorite, a condition of affairs which caused the other fourteen wives as little concern as their objections, if they had expressed any, would probably have caused their royal husband. So far as Ahmeya was concerned, she never minded a little thing like that, but included the last arrival in the same indifferent toleration which she had extended to her predecessors.

I saw the new wife only once.--I mean,--yes I mean that.--I saw her as the king's wife only once. She was a handsome woman, with a certain insolent disdain of those about her which indicated that she knew her own charms, and perhaps counted too much on their being permanent.

That summer my work took me away from the island. I went to Manila, and eventually to America. When I finally returned to Culion a year had passed.

I had engaged Mateo, before I left, to look out for such property as I left behind, and had retained my old house. I found him waiting for me, and with everything in good order. That is one good thing to be said about the natives. An imagined wrong or insult may rankle in their minds for months, until they have a chance to stab you in the back. They will lie to you at times with the most unblushing nerve, often when the truth would have served their ends so much better that it seems as if they must have been doing mendacious gymnastics simply to keep themselves in practice; but they will hardly ever steal. If they do, it will be sometime when you are looking squarely at them, carrying a thing off from under your very nose with a cleverness which they seem to think, and you can hardly help feel yourself, makes them deserve praise instead of blame. I have repeatedly left much valuable property with them, as I did in this case with Mateo, and have come back to find every article just as I had left it.

Mateo was glad to see me. "Oh Senor," he began, before my clothes were fairly changed, and while he was settling my things in my bed room, "there is so much to tell you."

I knew he would be bursting with news of what had happened during my absence. "Such goings on," he continued, folding my travelling clothes into a tin trunk, where the white ants could not get at them. "You never heard the likes of it."

I am translating very freely, for I have noticed that the thoughts expressed by the Philippine gossip are very similar to those of his fellow in America, or Europe, or anywhere else, no matter how much the words may differ.

"The new Sultana, the handsome Visayan girl, has given birth to a son, and has so bewitched the Sultan by her good looks and craftiness that he has decreed her son, and not Ahmeya's, to be the heir to the throne. She rules the palace now, and when her servants bear her through the streets the people bow down to her." He added, with a look behind him to see that no one overheard, "Because they dare not do otherwise. In their hearts they love Ahmeya, and hate this vain woman."

"How does Ahmeya take it?" I asked.

"Hardly, people think, although she makes no cry. She goes not through the streets of the town, now, but stays shut in her own rooms, with her women and the boy."

A furious beating against the bamboo walls of my sleeping room, and wild cries from some one on the ground outside, awoke me one morning when I had been back in Culion less than a week. The house in which I slept, like most of the native houses in the Philippines, was built on posts, several feet above the ground, for the sake of coolness and as a protection against snakes and such vermin.

It was very early, not yet sunrise. A servant of the Sultan's, gray with fright, was pounding on the walls of the house with a long spear to wake me, begging me, when I opened the lattice, to come to the palace at once.

I thought the monarch must have had some terrible attack, and wondered what it could be, but while we were hurrying up the street the messenger managed to make me understand that the Sultan was not at the palace at all, but gone the day before on board the royal proa for a state visit to a neighboring island from which he exacted yearly tribute. Later I learned that he had tried to have the Visayan woman go with him, but that she had wilfully refused to go. What was the matter at the palace the ruler being gone, I could not make out. When I asked this of the man who had come for me, he fell into such a palsy of fear that he could say nothing. When I came to know, later, that he was the night guard at the palace, and remembered what he must have seen, I did not wonder.

At the palace no one was astir. The man had come straight for me, stopping to rouse no one else. I had saved the Sultan's life. At least he thought so. Might I not do even more?

My guide took me straight through the first court yard, and down the narrow passage into the inner yard, around which were built the apartments of the woman. Ahmeya, I knew, lived in the rooms at one end of the square. The man led me towards the opposite end of the enclosure. Beside an open door he stood aside for me to enter, saying, as he did so, "Senor, help us."

The sun had risen, now, and shining full upon a lattice in the upper wall, flooded the room with a soft clear light.

The body of the Visayan woman, or rather what had been a body, lay on the floor in the center of the room, a shapeless mass of crushed bones and flesh. An enormous python lay coiled in one corner. His mottled skin glistened in the morning light, but he did not move, and his eyes were tight shut, as were those of the "green devil" after I had seen him feed.

I looked backward, across the court yard. The door of the big bamboo cage beneath the trees was open. I turned to the room again and looked once more. I knew now why the night guard's face was ash-colored, and why he could not speak.

For the child of the Visayan woman I could not see.

"OUR LADY OF PILAR"

How very singular! What do you suppose they are doing?"

"I'm sure I don't know. The American mind is unequal to grappling with the problem of what the natives are doing out here, most of the time. They seem to be praying. Or are they having a thanksgiving?"

"I don't know. All women, too!"

The young American woman and the officer who was her escort halted their horses to watch better the group of people of whom they had been speaking. The officer was a lieutenant of the American forces stationed in Zamboanga, the oldest and most important city in Mindanao, the headquarters of the United States military district in the Philippines known as the Department of Mindanao and Jolo. The young woman was the daughter of one of the older officers of the department, just come to Zamboanga the day before, and in this morning's ride having her first chance to see the strange old city to which her father had been transferred from Manila a few weeks before.

In the course of this ride the young people had reached Fort Pilar, at one end of the town, a weather-beaten old fortification built years and years before by the Spaniards as a protection against their implacable foes, the Moros, who waged continual warfare against them from the southern islands of the archipelago. Circling the stone walls of the fort the riders had come upon a group of as many as fifty Visayan women kneeling on the ground, their faces turned devoutly toward a stone tablet let into the walls.

An American soldier was doing sentry duty not far away. "Wait here, Miss Allenthorne," Lieutenant Chickering said, "and I'll find out from that man over there what they are doing. He's been here long enough so that probably he knows by this time." The officer cantered his pony over to the sentry's station. The American girl, left to herself, slipped down from her pony, and hooking the bridle rein into her elbow, walked a little nearer to the women. They did not seem to mind her in the least, and one of them--a handsome young woman near her--when she looked up and saw that the stranger was an American, smiled, and said something in a language which Miss Allenthorne did not understand; but from the expression on her face the American felt sure that what the woman said was meant as a welcome.

Something which this Visayan woman did a moment later excited Miss Allenthorne's curiosity to a still higher pitch. The native woman drew a small photograph from the folds of her "camisa," and kissed it. Then she put it down on the ground between herself and the wall, and turned to the tablet above it a face lighted with a radiance which any woman seeing would have known could have come from love alone. When she had finished, and had risen to her feet, she saw that the young American "senorita" was still watching her.

The two woman had been born with the earth between them, and with centuries of difference in traditions and training. Neither could understand the words which the other spoke, but when their eyes met there went from the heart of each to the heart of the other a message which did not require words to make itself understood.

With a beautiful grace of manner and expression, the Visayan went to the other woman, and again speaking as if she thought her words could be understood, held out the picture which she had kissed, for the stranger to look at.

The photograph was that of a young American officer, in a lieutenant's uniform.

Grace Allenthorne and her mother had lived in Manila for several months. As the daughter of one of the oldest and most highly respected officers in the service, and as a beautiful and attractive young woman, she had naturally been popular in the life of the military element of Manila's society. If she had herself been asked to describe the situation in Manila, Grace would have said that she liked no one officer better than another. They had all been "so nice" to her. With the exception of two of their number, however, the officers with whom she had ridden and talked and danced, would have said, if they had expressed their opinion of the matter, that they were all out of it except Lieutenant Chickering and Lieutenant Day; and some of them, among themselves, possibly may have made quiet bets as to which one of these two men would win in the end.

Then there came one of those official wavings of red tape in the air, which army officers' families learn to dread as signals of approaching trouble, and Colonel Allenthorne was transferred from Luzon to Mindanao; and among the troops sent with him were the companies of the rival lieutenants.

When the General sent back word that Zamboanga was a quiet city, with a fair climate and comfortable quarters, his wife and daughter followed him. If either of the young officers flattered himself that Grace was coming on his account, and that he was going to be made aware of her preference for himself on her arrival in Mindanao, he was disappointed.

Lieutenant Chickering was on duty when Miss Allenthorne arrived, and she devoted two hours that evening to hearing Lieutenant Day describe the city as he had found it. The next morning Lieutenant Day was on duty, and she went to ride with Lieutenant Chickering, possibly to learn if the information she had been favoured with the night before had been correct.

Lieutenant Chickering cantered back from the sentry's post. Finding his companion dismounted, he jumped down from his own pony and came to join her. The native woman had gone her way toward the city before he returned, smiling a good-bye to Miss Allenthorne when she found that her words were not understood, and hiding the photograph in her bosom as she turned to go.

"I've found out all about it, Miss Allenthorne," the Lieutenant exclaimed.

"There is a story which it seems the natives believe, that years ago there was once, where we now stand, a river which ran down past the fort and emptied into the sea. To give access to this river there was then a gate in the wall of the fort, directly opposite where we are now. Over the gate was a marble statue of a saint, who was called 'Our Lady of Pilar.'

"One night a soldier who was on sentry duty at the gate saw a white figure pass out before him. He challenged it, and when he got no answer challenged again and again. When the third summons brought no response, he aimed his gun at the figure and fired.

"In the morning this sentry was found at his post, stone dead, and the statue of the saint was gone. What was still more strange, the river which had always flowed past the gate had dried up in the night, and has never been seen since. After a time they built up the gate into a solid part of the wall, as you see it now; because as there was then no river here, there was no need of the gate. This had hardly been done when the tablet which we see there now made its appearance miraculously. All these strange manifestations attracted so much attention to the place that this shrine was set up here, and now for years it has been a favourite place for devout worshippers--especially women--to come to pray and to give thanks for blessings which they have received.

"It's interesting, isn't it?"

"Very," assented Miss Allenthorne, when the officer had finished; and then she added, almost immediately, "Don't you think it's getting very warm? Wouldn't we better ride back now?"

"Just as you say," the officer answered. Then he helped her to mount, mounted his own horse, and they rode home.

That evening Miss Allenthorne was invisible. When Lieutenant Day called, her mother explained that the young woman had a headache, possibly from riding too far in the sun that morning.

Alone in her room the young woman heard the officer's inquiry and her mother's excuses, for the bamboo walls of a Philippine house let conversation be heard from one end of the house to the other. Crushing in both hands the handkerchief which she had been dipping into iced water to bind about her forehead, she flung it impatiently from her, thinking bitterly to herself as she did so how foolish it was to bind up one's head when it was really one's heart that was aching.

For alone in her darkened room that afternoon, the young woman had acknowledged to herself--what perhaps up to that time had been almost as much of a problem to her as to other people--which one of the young officers she really cared for. She knew now that the love of Lieutenant Day meant everything to her, and the love of the other man nothing.

And it was Lieutenant Day's picture which she had seen the Visayan woman kiss.

One day General Allenthorne sat on the verandah of his house with an American acquaintance, the agent of a business firm, who had been sent to the Philippine Islands to see what opportunities there might be for trade there.

Some women walked along the street below the house, carrying heavy water jars poised on their heads.

"Queer country, isn't it?" said the visitor.

"Yes," said the General. "A body never knows what may happen to him. Probably those women we see down there are slaves. Seeing them made me think of a funny thing I heard of today, which happened to one of my men a little while ago.

"A young officer hired a native man for a servant. One day the fellow came to the Lieutenant in a great state of mind, begging the officer to help him. It seemed he had a sweetheart who was a Visayan slave girl owned by a Moro. The man who owned the girl was going to leave the city and take all his property, including this slave girl, with him. Pedro--that was the officer's boy--wanted 'the great American Senor' to say she should not go. Some of the natives seem to have the most wonderful confidence in the power of the Americans to do anything and everything.

"The officer told his boy he had no power to prevent the man's moving and taking his property with him; but he happened to ask how much the girl was worth. How much do you think the fellow said? Fifteen dollars! And he went on to explain that this was an unusually high price, he knew, but that this girl was young and handsome and clever at work. Of course he thought so, for he was in love with her.

"Well, I suppose the Lieutenant was flush, or felt generous, or perhaps something had happened to put him in an unusually serene frame of mind. He handed over fifteen dollars, and told Pedro to go and buy the girl and marry her; which he did, and has been the happiest man alive ever since. He is really grateful, too, and there isn't another officer in the service that is waited on as Lieutenant Day is. The funniest part of it all is, though, that he just found out a day or two ago, that in his gratitude Pedro had stolen one of his master's photographs to give to the Visayan girl he had married, so that she could see what their benefactor looked like, and she has been going out with it every day to an altar, or shrine, or something of that sort in the wall of an old fort here, where the native women go to worship, to pray to the saint there to shower all kinds of blessings on the American Senor who brought all this happiness to her and her husband.

"The boys have guyed Day so much about it, since they found it out, that he swears he will discharge the man, and have him hauled up for stealing the picture into the bargain. If he does, the woman will be likely to think that there is something the matter with the saint, I reckon, or that her prayers havn't found favour."

For once the wicker walls of a bamboo house had a merit all their own. At least that was what a certain young woman thought, when she could not help hearing this conversation in the room in which she had shut herself for the afternoon.

That night at dinner Miss Grace Allenthorne, was so radiant that even her father noticed it.

"What have you been doing, Grace?" he said. "What's the reason you feel so well, tonight? I havn't seen you look so fine for a month."

"Oh, nothing, father," said the girl. "I don't know of any special reason. I think that you just imagine it."

Which was, of course, a very wrong thing for her to say; for she knew perfectly well what the reason was.

While they were still at table a messenger came post haste for General Allenthorne, with word that he was wanted at once at headquarters. He was absent nearly all night.

In the morning it was known that an outpost in the northern part of the island had been surprised and almost captured. The enemy was still in force about the place and threatening it. A loyal native had crept through the lines to bring word and ask for help. A relief force had been made up and sent at once. Lieutenant Day was among those who volunteered to go, and had gone.

Ten days of horrible anxiety followed. Then word came that the relief party had reached the post in time. The forces surrounding the place had been scattered, and the post was safe. There had been a sharp fight, though, and among those who had been badly wounded was Lieutenant Day.

Of course he got well. No man could help it, with four such nurses as Mrs. Allenthorne and Mrs. Allenthorne's daughter Grace, and Pedro and Pedro's Visayan wife Anita.

Just what Grace told her mother, which led that worthy person to become responsible for the young officer's recovery, no one ever knew except the two women themselves, but in addition to being a motherly-hearted woman, Mrs. Allenthorne was a soldier's daughter as well as a soldier's wife, so perhaps it was not necessary to explain so many things to her as it would have been to some people.

Nobody ever knew--or at least never told--what explanation the young woman made to the Lieutenant, when he came back to consciousness and found her helping to care for him. Perhaps she did not explain. Possibly the explanations made themselves, or else none were needed.

At any rate, the young man got well, and since then he has been known to say--although this was in the strictest confidence to a very particular person--that he should always regard the Visayan woman's prayers before "Our Lady of Pilar" with the profoundest gratitude, because the greatest blessing of his whole life had come to him through this woman's praying for him outside the walls of the old fort.

A QUESTION OF TIME

The native pilot who is to take the gunboat Utica around from Ilo Ilo to Capiz is a traitor. I have just discovered indisputable proofs of that fact. He has agreed to run the gunboat aground on a ledge near one of the Gigantes Islands, on which a force of insurgents is to be hidden, large enough to overpower the men on the gunboat in her disabled condition. Do not let her leave Ilo Ilo until you have a new pilot, and one you are sure of.

"Demauny."

Captain James Demauny, of the American army in the Philippine Islands, folded the dispatch which he had just written, and sealed it. Then, calling an orderly to him he said, "Send Sergeant Johnson to me."

Captain Demauny's company was then at Pasi, a small inland town in the island of Panay. He had been dispatched by the American general commanding at Ilo Ilo, the chief seaport of Panay, to march to Capiz, a seaport town on the opposite side of the island, to assist from the land side a small force of Americans besieged there by the natives, while the gunboat Utica was to steam around the northeastern promontory of the island and cooperate from the water side of the town, in its relief.

The distance across the island was about fifty miles, while that by water, by the route which the Utica must traverse, was about two hundred miles. Captain Demauny, starting first, had covered half the march laid out for him, without incident, until, halting at Pasi, half way across the island and well up in the mountains, he had been so fortunate as to obtain the information which he was about to send back to the commander at Ilo Ilo. Panay had been, up to this time, one of the most quiet islands in the group. He had met with no opposition in his march, so far, and it was believed that the only natives on the island who were under arms were those living in the northeastern part of the territory. It was a force of these that had invested Capiz.

"Sergeant Johnson, sir," the orderly reported.

"Very well. Send him in."

A young man, wearing a faded brown duck uniform, tightly buttoned leggings, and a wide-rimmed gray hat, entered the tent.

"I have sent for you, sergeant," said Captain Demauny, "for two reasons. One is that I want a man who is brave, and one whom I can trust."

The sergeant bent his head slightly, in acknowledgement of the implied compliment, his cheeks looking a trifle darker shade of brown, where the blood had flushed the skin beneath its double deep coat of tan.

"The other reason," the officer went on, "is that I want a man of whose muscle and endurance as a runner, and whose skill as a boatman, I have had some proof."

In spite of the difference in rank, and the seriousness of the situation, which the officer knew and the man guessed, the two men looked at each other and smiled. For one was a Harvard man, and the other had come from Yale.

"The gunboat Utica is to leave Ilo Ilo at midnight, tonight. It is of the very greatest importance that this dispatch," handing him the letter, "be delivered to the American general at Ilo Ilo before the vessel gets under way. I entrust it to you, to see that it is delivered.

"You ought to have no trouble in getting there in ample season," the captain continued, spreading out a map so that the other man could see it. "I cannot spare any men for an escort for you, because my force is already far too small for what we have to do. Instead of following back the road we took in coming here--which would be impassable for any one but a man on foot, even if I had a horse for you, which I have not--I think you can make better time by another route.

"Six miles from here," pointing to the map, "you will reach the same river which we crossed at a point farther up the stream. Get a boat there and go down the river some fifteen or twenty miles, until you come to a native village built at the head of steep falls in the stream. I am told that until you reach there the river is navigable, and that the current is so swift much of the way that you can make rapid progress. At that village you will have to leave your boat, but from that place you will find a clearly marked path to Ilo Ilo.

"The quicker you start, the better; and, as I have told you, I trust it to you to see that the general has the dispatch before the Utica leaves port."

It was ten o'clock in the forenoon when the sergeant had been sent for to come to headquarters. Half an hour later he had started, the letter tightly wrapped in a bit of rubber blanket before he had placed it inside his jacket, for he had already had enough experience with the native boats to know how unstable they would be in the current of a rapid river.

The five miles from Pasi to the river were easily made, in spite of the fact that it was midday, for there was a good path, which, for nearly all the distance, was shaded by lofty trees. When he reached the river the sergeant bought from a man whom he found there a native "banca," for three dollars, a sum of money which would make a native rich. In this boat he started on his voyage down the river.

A native "banca" is a "dug-out," a canoe hollowed out from the trunk of a tree. It is propelled and guided by a short, broad-bladed paddle, and is as unstable as the lightest racing shell, although not any where nearly so easy to send through the water.

It was unfortunate for the sergeant that he did not know--what he could not, since the map did not show it--that the place where the path touched the river first was on the upper side of a huge "ox-bow" bend. If he had kept on by land, a third of a mile's walk farther through the swamp would have brought him to the river again, at a point to reach which by water, following the river's windings, he would have to paddle three or four miles.

Another thing which was unfortunate; that he could not know the nature of the man from whom he bought the "banca," any better than he could know the nature of the river, and so did not suspect that he was dealing with a "tulisane," to whom the little bag of money which the officer had shown when he had paid for the boat had looked like boundless wealth, to see which was to plan to possess.

A "tulisane" is to the Philippine Islands what a brigand is to Italy, a bandit to Spain, a highwayman to England, and a train-robber to America; a man who lives by his wits, and stops at no means to gain his object. The "banca," by the way, was stolen property.

This man would have stabbed the American soldier when he stooped to step cautiously into the slippery boat, and taken the purse from his dead body, had he not been far-sighted enough to see that the purse might be had, and much more money beside.

The "tulisane" knew that the American soldiers were at Pasi. Although he did not find it best to come to town himself, in general, he never had any trouble finding men to go there for him, and bring him news, or carry messages. No bandit leader who promptly carves an ear off the man who does his errands grudgingly is half so feared as a Filipino "tulisane" whom his fellows know to be the possessor of a powerful "anting-anting." And this man's "anting-anting" was famous for the wonders which it had done.

The "tulisane" knew that the American soldiers were at Pasi; and that the man who led them lived in one of the white tents they had set up there. This man in the brown clothes, which looked so tight that it made the Filipino tired just to look at them, could be no common soldier, else he would not be paying three big silver dollars for a "banca." If anything was to happen to this man--that is if he was to disappear, and still not be dead, and the officer in the white tent should know of it--the leader of the white soldiers would no doubt pay much money to have his man brought safely back. Consequently the man in the brown clothes, with the fat money purse, should be made to disappear.

That was the way the "tulisane" reasoned. It was the three dollars, the rest of the money in the purse, and the ransom which the leader of the white men would pay, which influenced the Filipino. It was not that the Asiatic highwayman cared a leaf of a forest tree for patriotism. So long as he got the money, white men and brown men were all alike to him, American soldiers and Filipino insurgents.

So the native, going into the forest, a little way back from the river, looked until he found a tree the roots of which growing out from well up the trunk had made a sort of great wooden drum. Taking a stout stick of hard wood which had been leaned against the tree,--he had been there before,--he struck the hollow tree three heavy blows, the sound of which went echoing off through the forest. Then the man listened.

Not long; for from far, very far away, there came an answer, one blow, and then, after a moment's pause, two more. The drum beats which followed, and the pauses for the faint replies, were like listening to a giant's telegraph.

The soldier, paddling steadily out around the river's winding course, heard the noise and wondered curiously what it was. The natives who heard it said, "The trees are talking," meaning that some one was making them talk. To the "tulisane" the sounds meant that he was bringing his partner to help him, just as at night the far-off, long-drawn cry of a panther calls the creature's mate to share the prey.

Sergeant Johnson, still paddling, after he would have said that with the help of the current he had put four good miles of the river behind him, saw a tiny ripple in the water ahead of the boat, but in a stream so rapid thought nothing of it.

An instant later a cocoanut fibre rope, stretched taut across the river and just below the surface of the water, had turned his skittish boat bottom upward. The "tulisane," you see, had seen the sergeant's revolver, and thought wisest to attack him wet.

Drenched, blowing for breath, before he knew what had happened, the soldier found himself dragged to the bank, disarmed, robbed, his hands bound behind him, and his feet hobbled. He could speak Spanish and so could the "tulisanes." Words told him that his captors, only two in number, meant him to march, hobbled as he was, along a path which they pointed out; but it took several sharp pricks from a "campilan" which one of them carried, to make him start. For the path led away from the river, away from Pasi, from Ilo Ilo and the Utica, which he would have given his life itself rather than fail to reach in time.

Only a little way back from the river the path began to leave the low land, mounting up to the hills among which the "tulisanes" had their camp. Sometimes one of the brigands led the way, with the prisoner between them, sometimes both drove him before them, secure in the knowledge that in his helpless condition he could not escape. The captain's message, in its rubber case, still lay undisturbed and dry within the messenger's jacket. For that he was glad, although his heart sank as every step carried him farther away from the destination of the dispatch, and from the chance of its being delivered in season.

The means which providence uses to accomplish the ends which it desires are marvellous, and those of us who do not believe in providence say, "a strange coincidence."

The day before, back among the mountains of Panay, a little old Montese woman, who had never heard of God, or of America, and whose only dress had been thirty yards of fine bamboo plaiting coiled round and round her body, had died.

When the dead body had been set properly upright beneath the tiny hut which had been the woman's home, and food and drink placed beside it for the long journey which the spirit was to take, the hut was abandoned, as is the custom of the tribe, and the men of the family, the woman's sons and nephews, started out with freshly sharpened lances and "mechetes."

For this is the only religion of the Monteses; that no one must be left to go alone upon the long journey. And so, when one of a family dies, the men relatives do not stay their hands until some one,--the first person met,--is slain by them to go on the journey as an escort. Only if they seek three days through the wood, and find no human being, then, after the third day, a beast may be slain, and the law of blood still be satisfied.

The sons and nephews of the Montese woman had marched for thirty-six hours, and the steel of their weapons had not been dimmed by any moisture other than the dew, when, suddenly rounding a turn in the mountain path, they met three men.

The first of the three at that moment was the "tulisane" leader, and him, in thirty seconds, they had driven six lances through. His partner, with a scream of terror, dashed into the trackless forest and disappeared. He need not. The demand for a sacrifice was appeased, and the men who had killed the "tulisane" cared as little for his companion as they did for the white man who had been his prisoner. All they wanted, now, was to get back to the Montese country, and to the new huts which their women would have been building in their absence. The white man's words they could not understand, but his gestures were intelligible, and before they parted, he to hurry back towards the river and they towards the Montese country, they had cut the cords which bound the soldier's hands and hobbled his feet, and thus had left him free to make such haste as he could.

Even then the afternoon was well nigh gone when the messenger reached the river at the place where he had been dragged from it; and practically all his journey was yet before him, wearied as he was.

For once, though, fortune favored him. His dug-out had grounded on a sandy island hardly a dozen rods below where it had been overturned, and swimming out to it, he soon had righted it and was on his way again.

At first the forest on each side was a tropic swamp. Then the river grew more swift, with here and there rapids in which it took all his skill with his clumsy paddle to keep his boat from being upset. The ground had begun to grow higher here, and back from the banks there were rank growths of hemp and palm trees.

A few miles farther, and he was in the mountains, the river winding about like a lane of water between walls which were almost perpendicular, and covered with the densest, bright green foliage, in which parrots croaked hoarsely and monkeys chattered sleepily as they settled themselves for the night. The walls of the living canon grew narrower and steeper. The river here was as still as a lake, and the current so sluggish that only his labour with the paddle sent the "banca" forward. It grew dark quickly and fast, down in the bottom of this mountain gorge, and by and by the twilight glow on the tops of the banks, when he would peer up at them, grew fainter.

The soldier strained his eyes to look ahead. Would the living green canons of that river never end? It was dark now, except that the stars in the narrow line of sky above the gorge sent down light enough to make the surface of the water gleam faintly and mark out his course.

He drew his paddle from the water, and holding it so that the drops which trickled from it would make no noise, listened breathlessly for the sound of the falls which marked the site of the village he was to find, and at it leave his boat for the land again. A night bird screamed in the forest, and then there was utter silence, until a soft splash in the water beside him revealed the ugly head of a huge black crocodile following the dug-out.

By and by the stars in the lane of sky above grew dim, and a stronger light, which faintly illuminated the river gorge, told him that the full moon had risen, although not yet high enough to light his course directly. After a time the gorge grew wider and its sides less steep and high; and then, at last, he heard the roar of the falls, and found the village, and had landed.

What time it might be now the sergeant did not dare to guess. A sleepy native pointed out to him the path, stared, when the stranger said he must hurry on to Ilo Ilo that night, and flatly refusing to be his guide, went back to bed.

The forest path was rankly wet with night dew, and dimly lighted by the moon. The soldier hurried forward, only to find that in his haste he had missed the main path. Slowly and anxiously he retraced his way until he found the right road again, and then went forward slowly enough now to go with care.

And so, at last, he saw before him the city of Ilo Ilo, only to learn, when he was challenged by a picket, that it was one o'clock and that the Utica had steamed out of the harbour an hour before.

Useless as he feared the dispatch might be now, Sergeant Johnson insisted that it be delivered at once, and that he be given an opportunity to ask to be allowed to tell the general why he was so late. When that officer, roused from sleep, had read the dispatch and heard the story briefly, for there were other things to be thought of then, he told the young man, "You have done well," for he knew the ways of Filipino "tulisanes," "and after all perhaps you may not be too late."

But before he explained what he meant by the last part of his sentence, the general called for one of his aids, and as soon as the man could be brought, hastily gave him certain orders with instructions that they were to be communicated to the officers whom they concerned, as quickly as was possible, regardless of how sound asleep those gentlemen might be.

Then, because he was at heart a kindly man, and because he felt that the water-soaked, thorn-torn soldier before him, pale with weariness and anxiety, had done his best, the general told him what was the nature of the dispatch, and why, even then, he might yet be in time.

For by another of the fortunate dispensations of providence, or if you please, by a strange coincidence, that very afternoon another American gunboat had unexpectedly steamed into the harbour of Ilo Ilo and dropped anchor.

The general had sent messages to the commander of the Ogdensburgh, explaining the situation to him, and as soon as that officer understood the matter he replied, "You did just right."

"We will start in pursuit of the Utica as soon as we can get up steam, and do our best to overtake her."

Could they overtake her? That was the question. She had a good three hours start, for daylight was breaking before the Ogdensburgh could be got under way, and the registered speed of the boats was about equal.

At any rate there was doubt enough as to what the result would be so that when the Ogdensburgh reached the town of Concepcion, fifty miles up the coast from Ilo Ilo, and the Utica was seen to be lying at anchor in the harbour there, the commander of the Ogdensburgh said words which were as thankful as they were emphatic. For just beyond Concepcion harbour began the narrow channels of the

Gigantes Islands, in some of which he had feared to find the gunboat wrecked.

When the captain of the Utica came to know why he was pursued, and what he had escaped, he was as grateful for the faulty cylinder head which had delayed him as, the night before, he had been exasperated by it.

The pilot, charged with his treachery, proved at once that the charge was true, by turning traitor again and offering to buy the safety of his own neck by guiding the boats to where they could shell the woods in which the natives were hidden.

THE SPIRIT OF MT. APO

From the deck of any vessel passing up the southeast coast of Mindanao, the voyager can see the gold-crowned summit of Apo, rising like a gilded cone high above the dense vegetation of the island at its base.

Next to Luzon, on which the city of Manila is situated, Mindanao is the largest of all the islands of the Philippine archipelago. Lying as it does far to the southeast, and near the Sulu Islands, the Moros, as the venturesome Sulus are called, invaded Mindanao more than two hundred years ago, and gradually crept farther and farther along the coasts and up the river valleys, waging intermittent warfare against the Visayans who had come from the west to settle on the island, and against the natives that lived inland, and keeping up constant relentless war upon the Spaniards who claimed the sovereignty of the island. There are few islands of its size in the world where so many different kinds of people live, and perhaps no other where so many wild deeds have been done. Until within the last two years, a man's will there has been likely to be his only law.

Nature has done much for the island. The soil is of incalculable richness. Fruits and grains grow luxuriantly where the ground is turned over, and as if to make the natives laugh at the need of such labour the forests yield fruits and nuts with lavish generosity. Deer and buffalo run wild, and numberless varieties of pigeons live in the trees.

Mount Apo, in the extreme southeastern part of the island, and almost upon the coast, is the loftiest mountain in the archipelago. Its height is usually estimated to be not far from ten thousand feet. A spiral of steam drifting up from the sulphur-crowned summit of the mountain shows that fires still linger in its bosom, but for many years it has been quiet, and at no time does history show that it has broken forth in fury to wreak the awful destruction that is written down against some of the volcanoes of these islands.

My work as a naturalist had several times brought me where I could see Apo, and each time I had been more and more fascinated by it, and more desirous of climbing to its top.

When I began to talk of making the ascent, though, I found it would be no easy matter. Not only were the sides of the mountain said to be steep, and the forests which clothed them impassable, but there were mysterious dangers to be encountered. Men who had gone with me anywhere else I had asked them, had affairs of their own to attend to when I spoke of climbing Apo, or else flatly refused to go.

I was told that no man that started up the mountain had ever come back. Enormous pythons drew their green bodies over its sides. Man-apes lived in its upper forests whose strength no human being could meet. Devils and goblins lurked in the crevasses below the summit, and above all and most terrible of all, there was a spirit of the mountain whose face to see was death.

My questions as to how they knew all these things if no man had lived to come back from the mountain had no effect. This was not a case for logic; it was one of those where instinct ruled.

There is a queer little animal, something like a sable, which is peculiar to Mindanao. The natives call it "gato del monte," which means "mountain cat." I wanted to get some specimens of this animal and also of a variety of pigeon which they call "the stabbed dove," because it has a tuft of bright red feathers like a splash of blood upon its otherwise snow-white breast.

To get these I settled myself in a native village a few miles inland from the town of Dinagao, on the west shore of the Gulf of Davao. Mount Apo towered just above this place, and I meant to climb its sides before I left the valley.

After the Bagabos in whose village I was living found that all their tales of the terrible dangers on Apo did not dissuade me from tempting them, three of the men agreed to pilot me as far up the mountain side as they ever went, and to carry there for me a sufficient supply of food to last me, as they evidently believed, as long as I should need food. One of them, the best guide and carrier I had found on the whole island, had screwed his courage up to where he had promised to go farther with me; but the morning of our start a "quago" bird flew across our path and hooted; and that settled the matter. Such an ominous portent as that no intelligent Bagabo could be expected to disregard. The men hardly could be got to carry my luggage as far as they had agreed, and as soon as they had put the things down, they bade me a hasty farewell and scuttled down the mountain as fast as their legs could carry them.

I slept that night where the men had left me, and set out early the next morning, hoping to get to the top of the mountain and back to the same place before night overtook me. The climb was more than hard for the first mile--harder than I had even feared. The forest grew so dense as to be practically impassable, and I finally took to the bed of a rocky stream, up which the travelling, although dangerous, was not so hard.

In time, though, by scrambling up this water course, I passed beyond the tree line, and then, where there was only shrubbery, it was fairly easy to get along. I could see above the vegetation, now, and the view even from here would have repaid me for all my effort. The side of the mountain swept down in a majestic curve from my feet to the sea. At its base was Dinagao, and farther up the coast, Davao. Beyond them lay the blue waters of the Gulf of Davao, and far across this, showing only as a line of deeper blue upon the water, the mountain ranges of the eastern peninsula.

The bushes through which I waded were bent down with the ripe berries which grew on them. A herd of small, dark brown deer feeding among the bushes hardly moved out of my way. I wondered at their tameness, but thought it must be because no man had ever come within their sight before.

Above the bushes there was a zone of rock, broken in places into huge boulders, and then between this and the cone was the sulphur field, glowing, now that I was near enough to see it, with a richness of colouring such as no painter's palette could reproduce. From darkest green to deepest blue, through all the tints and shades of yellow, the colour scheme went, with here and there a touch of rose.

I had stopped a moment to get breath and to gaze at the wonderful scene before me when there came into it and stood still between two great rocks, as a living picture might have stepped up into its frame, a woman, the strangest to look at that I have ever seen.

She was young and slender. She was dressed in a simple, dark-brown, hemp-cloth garment which fell from neck to feet, and her round young arms were bare to the shoulder.

It took me a full minute, before I could realize what it was which made her look so strange to me.

Then I knew. It had been so long since I had seen a white woman that I did not know one when I saw her.

This woman's face and arms were as white as mine--much whiter, indeed, for I was tanned by months of Asiatic sun--and the hair which fell about her shoulders and down below her waist, was white;--not light, or golden, but white.

For once in my life, I am willing to confess, my nerves went back on me; and I could think of nothing but what the natives in the village at the foot of the mountain had told me. Pythons and man-apes and devils I had seen no trace of, but here, beyond question, was the "Spirit of the Mountain."

A stout, pointed staff of iron-wood, which I had been carrying to help me in my scramble up the mountain, slipped from my hand and fell clattering to the rocks. The woman turned her head toward the spot from which the sound had come, as if she heard the noise of the stick upon the stones, but although we were only a little way from each other, there was no expression in her face to indicate that she saw me.

Then she spoke.

"Madre!"

There was no answer, and she called again, clearer and louder.

"Ma-dre!"

There was a sound of swift steps on the stones, and a moment later another woman--an older woman--came from behind one of the rocks.

As if in answer to some question in the girl's face, the woman looked down and saw me.

In an instant she had sprung before the younger woman, as if to hide her from me.

There are some women in the world whose very manner carries with it an impression of power. Such was the woman whom I saw before me now. Not young; dark of skin, clad only in the simplest possible hemp-cloth garment, there was in her face a dignity which could not but win instant recognition.

"Who are you?" she asked in Spanish. "And why do you come here?"

I told her as simply and as plainly as I could, who I was, and why I had come up the mountain. She kept her place in front of the girl, screening her from sight during all the time that we were talking.

When I had finished she stood silent for a moment, as if thinking what to do.

"Since you have come here," she said at last, "where I had thought no one would ever come, and have learned what I had hoped no one would ever know, you will not, I feel sure, deny me an opportunity to tell you enough of the reason why two women live in this wild place, so that I hope you will help them to keep their secret. May I ask you to go with us to the place which we call home?"

I said I would be glad to go, without having the slightest idea where we were going. I should have said it just the same, I think, if I had known she was going to lead me straight down into the crater of the volcano.

"Elena," the older woman said, speaking to the girl. Then she said something else, in a native dialect which I did not understand.

The girl came out from the place where she had been hidden, and passed behind the rocks. When I saw her face, now, I saw what I had not perceived before. She was blind.

When the girl had been gone a little time the woman said: "Will you follow me?"

She waited until I had climbed up to where she stood, and then led the way around the rock behind which the girl had disappeared. A well defined path led from that place down into the dwarfed vegetation, and then, through that to the forest beyond. The girl was already some distance down this path, walking rather slowly, as blind people walk, but steadily, and with fingers outstretched here and there to touch the bushes on each side.

We followed. Where the trees began to be tall enough to furnish shelter, my guide stopped, pushed aside the branches of what appeared to be an impenetrable thicket, and motioned me to follow her through. The girl had disappeared again. The opening through which we went was so thoroughly hidden that I might have gone past it fifty times and never suspected it was there, or thought that the path down which we had come was anything but a deer track.

Another short path led us to a cleared space in the forest in which a long, low house of bamboo and thatch had been built. A herd of deer was feeding near the house. Those directly in our path moved lazily out of the way. The others did not stir. I knew then why the deer that I had seen as I had come up the mountain were so tame.

A broad porch was built against one side of the house, and under this were hung fibre hammocks. The woman pointed me to one of these hammocks, and leaving me there went into the house. When she came back she brought two gourds filled with some kind of home-made wine, and two wooden cups. The girl, coming just behind her, brought a basket of fruit which the woman took from her and placed upon a bamboo stand beside my hammock. Then, filling one of the cups from a gourd, she drank half its contents and set the cup down, fixing her eyes on mine as she did so.

I knew enough of native customs by this time to understand what this meant. If I took the cup which she had drunk from, and drank, I was a guest of the house, and bound in honor to do it no harm. If I poured wine from the other gourd into another cup and drank, I was under obligations as a guest only while I was under the roof.

I took the cup from the table and drank the half portion of wine which she had left in it.

"Thank you," the woman said. "I will trust you."

Then, sitting on a bamboo stool near my hammock, she began to talk. Only, at times, as she told me her story, she would rise and walk up and down the porch, as if she could tell some things easier walking than when sitting still.

Much of what she told me I shall not write down here; but enough for an understanding of the strange things which followed.

"My home was once in ----," she said, naming one of the most important towns in the island. "My father was a Spanish officer, rich, proud and powerful. My mother was a Visayan woman. When I was little more than a girl, my parents married me to a Spanish officer much older than myself. So far as I knew then what love was, I thought I loved him. Afterward, I came to know.

"Among the prisoners brought into my husband's care there came one day a Moro, whose life, for some reason, had been spared longer than was the lot of most prisoners. I told myself, the first time I saw this man, that he was the noblest looking man I had ever seen, and since that time I have never seen his equal. Chance made it possible for us to meet and speak, and then, in a little while, I came to know what love really is.

"One day I learned that the Moro prisoner was to be beheaded the next day. Word had come that a Spanish prisoner whom the Moros had captured some time before, and with the hope of whose ransom this man had been held, had been killed.

"That night"--the woman was walking the floor of the porch now--"I killed my husband while he was asleep, set the man I loved free, and we fled the city. By day we hid in the forests, and walked by night, until we came to a part of the island where the Moros lived. Nicomedis brought me to the town which had been his home, and we were married and lived there.

"Elena is our child. You have seen her."

I realized cow the truth about the girl;--her strange appearance, the color of her skin and eyes and hair. In my travels through the islands I had once or twice seen other albino children.

The woman had sat down again.

"Our life in the Moro town was never wholly comfortable. My husband's people distrusted me. I was of a different faith, and from a hostile race. They would rather he would have chosen a wife of his own people. When the child was born things grew worse. Some said the tribe would never win in war while the child lived;--it was a curse. Then came a year when the plague raged among the Moros as it had never been known to do, terrible as some of its visits before that time had been.

"One day a slave, whose life Nicomedis once had saved when his master would have beaten the man to death, came to our house and told us that the people of the town were coming to kill us all, that the curse might be removed and the plague stayed. My husband would have stood up to fight them all until he himself was killed, but for the sake of the child, and because I begged him not to leave us alone, he did not. Again we fled into the forest; and because the trees and the beasts and the birds were kinder to us than any men, we said we would come up here--where we knew no man dare come--and would live our lives here.

"Eight years ago my husband died." The woman was walking the porch again, and sometimes she waited a long time between the sentences of her story. "We buried him out there," pointing to where the forest came up to one side of the enclosure. "It is easy for us to live here. We have everything we need. We have never been disturbed before. Only once, years ago, did any of the natives come as far up the mountain as this, and it was easy for us to frighten them so that no one has dared to come since then. You are the only living person who knows our secret. Shall we know that it is to be safe with you?"

For answer I filled the wooden cup from the gourd again, drank half the contents, and handed the cup to her to drink the rest.

"I thank you," she said. "My life has had enough of sin and suffering in it so that I have hoped it may not have more of either.

"I would not have you think that I am complaining," she said hastily, a moment later, as if she was afraid I would get that impression. "I am not. I do not regret one day of my life. My hands are stained with what people call crime, and my heart knows all the weight which grief can lay upon a heart; but the joy of my life while my husband lived paid for it all. To have been loved by him as I was loved, was well worth crime and grief."

"Why do you not go away from here?" I asked. "Why not leave this country entirely, and go to some new land where you would be free from danger? I will help you to get away."

"We know nothing of other lands," she said. "We should be helpless there. We are better here." "Besides," a moment later, "his grave," pointing out toward the trees, "is here."

It had grown dark as we talked; the thick, dead darkness of a Philippine forest night. The deer on the ground outside the porch had lain down and curled their heads around beside them and gone to sleep. Enormous bats flew past the house. We could not see them, but we felt the air which their huge wings set in motion. The woman lighted a little torch of "viao" nuts. Elena came out of the house, walked across the porch and disappeared in the darkness, going toward the forest.

"Ought she to go?" I asked. "Will she not be lost, or hurt?"

"Did you not understand it all?" the girl's mother said. "She is blind only in the day time. At night she sees as readily as you and I do by day."

In a few minutes the girl came back with her hands filled with fresh picked fruit. She gave me this, and her mother brought out from the house such simple food as she could provide.

"You will sleep here, tonight," she said, and left me.

The next day I went to the top of the mountain, and after that, by making two trips to my camp, brought up all the articles which had been left there, including some blankets a gun and ammunition, some food and some medicines. These I asked "the woman of the mountain," as I called her to myself, to let me give to her. She took them, and thanked me. I stayed there that night, and the next day said good by to the two strange women, and went down the mountain.

When I reached my house in the village I found my neighbors getting ready to divide my property among themselves, since they were satisfied I would never return to claim it. They did not think it strange that I came back empty-handed. That I had come back at all was a wonder. For the sake of the security of the two women I let it be known that I had seen strange sights on the volcano's top, and that it was a perilous journey to climb its sides.

I planned to stay in the village some weeks longer. My house, like most of the native habitations, was built of bamboo, and was set upon posts several feet above the ground. I lived alone. One night about a month after my return, I woke from a sound sleep, choking.

Some one's hand was pressed tightly over my mouth, and another hand on my breast held me down motionless upon my sleeping mat.

"Don't speak!" some one whispered into my ear. "Don't make a sound! Lie perfectly quiet until you understand all that I am saying!

"The natives have banded themselves together to kill you tonight. They believe the village has been cursed ever since you came down from Mount Apo, and that you are the cause of it."

I could see now that there had been a growing coldness toward me on the part of the people ever since I had come back. And there had been evil luck, too. The chief's best horse had cast himself and had to be killed. Two men out hunting had fallen into the hands of a hostile tribe and been "boloed." Game had been unusually scarce, and a "quago" bird had hooted three nights in succession.

"They are coming here tonight to burn your house," the same voice whispered, "and kill you with their spears if you try to escape the flames. No matter how I knew, or how we came. There is no time to lose. You cannot stop to bring anything with you. Come outside the house at once, as noiselessly as possible, and Elena will lead us to where you can escape."

The hands were taken from my mouth and body, and I felt that I was alone.

A few moments later, outside the house, when I stepped from the ladder to the ground, a hand--a woman's hand--grasped mine firmly.

"Do not be afraid to follow," the same voice whispered. "Elena will lead the way, and will tell us of anything in the path."

The hand gave a tug at mine, and I followed. We were in absolute darkness. Sometimes the frond of a giant fern brushed against my cheek, or the sharp-pointed leaf of a palm stung my face, but that was all. The girl led us steadily onward through the forest.

"Stop!" she said, once, "and look back."

I turned my face in the direction from which we had come. A ray of light shone in the darkness, and quickly became a blaze. It was my house on fire. With the light of the fire came the sound of savage cries, the shouts of the men watching with poised spears about the burning house. In the dim light which the fire cast where we stood, I could make out the forms of my two companions. A black cloth bound around the girl's head hid her white hair. In the dark, her eyes, so blank in the day light, glowed like two stars. She held her mother by the hand, and the older woman's other hand grasped mine. I looked at the girl, and thought of Nydia, leading the fugitives from out Pompeii to safety.

Before the light of the fire had died, we were on our way again. It seemed to me as if we walked in the darkness of the forest for hours; but after a little we were following a beaten track. At times the girl told us to step over a tree fallen across the path, or warned us that we were to cross a stream. At last we came out on the hard sand of the ocean beach, and reached the water's edge. Freed from the forest's shade the darkness was less dense. I could make out the surface of the water, and out on it a little way some dark object. The girl spoke to her mother in their native tongue.

"There is a 'banca,'" the woman said, pointing out over the water to the boat. "No matter whose it is. Swim out to it, pull up the anchor, and before day comes you can be safe."

I tried to thank her.

"I am glad we could do it," she said, simply. "I am glad if we could do good."

Then they left me; and went back up the beach into the darkness.

WITH WHAT MEASURE YE METE

The story of the tax collector of Siargao reminds me of an official of that rank whom I once knew," said a fellow naturalist whom I once met at a club in Manila, and with whom I had been exchanging experiences. "It was when I was gathering specimens in Negros. They were a bad lot, those collectors, a set of money-grabbers of the worst kind, but, bad as they were, they had a hard time, too.

"If they did not make their pile, out of the poor natives, and go back to Manila or to Spain, rich, in three or four years, it was pretty likely to be because they had fallen victims to the hate of the natives or to the distrust of the officials at head-quarters.

"When I first went to Negros, and had occasion to go to the tribunal, as the government house was called, I noticed some objects in one of the rooms so odd and so different from anything I had seen anywhere else that I asked their use. I was told that they were used for catching men who had not paid their taxes.

"Among the various thorn-bearing plants which the swamps of the Philippine Islands produce is one called the 'bejuco,' or 'jungle rope.' This is a vine of no great size, but of tremendous strength, which, near the end, divides into several slender but very tough branches. Each of these branches is surrounded by many rings of long, wicked, recurved thorns, as sharp and strong as steel fish-hooks, and nearly as difficult to dislodge. The hunter who encounters a thicket of 'bejuco' goes around it, or turns back, for it is hopeless to try to go through. While he frees himself from the grasp of one thorn, a dozen more have caught him somewhere else.

"The objects which I had seen in the tribunal guard room were made of long bamboo poles, across one end of which two short pieces had been fastened. To these cross pieces were bound a great number of the 'bejuco' vines, so arranged that the innumerable hooks which they bore could be easily swung about in the air.

"The 'Gobernadorcillo' who was in office at the time was a man who had no mercy on his people. Negros, with the other islands of the group commonly known as Visayan, forms a province which is under the supervision of a governor who has his headquarters in the island of Cebu, where also the bishop who is the head of the see resides.

"Negros is near enough to Cebu so that the authority of the government could be maintained better there than it could in the more distant islands. When I was there the village of Dumaguete, the chief town and seaport of Negros, contained a stone fort, the most imposing probably of any outside the capital; while the garrison formed of half-breed soldiers who were on duty there, sent down from Cebu with the 'Gobernadorcillo,' kept the people in a degree of subjection which in many places would have been impossible.

"The men whom the Governor employed to round up his delinquent subjects were called 'cuadrilleros.' Sunday was the day he devoted to the sport, for such I think he really regarded it. The 'cuadrilleros' would start out in the morning with a list of the men who were wanted. A house would be surrounded, and unless the man had been given some warning of their coming, and had fled, he would be driven out. Then, if he tried to escape, or refused to come with them, one of the 'bejuco' 'man-catchers' was swung with a practiced hand in his direction, and, caught in a hundred places by its cruel, thorny hooks, he was led to town, the journey in itself being a torture such as few men would think they could endure. The whipping came later.

"It was not until Pedro fell into trouble that I came to know really the worst of all this. Of course I knew in a way, I had seen the 'bejuco' poles, and the rattans, and the whipping bench, and sometimes, of a Sunday, when I was in the village and could not go away, I had heard cries from the tribunal such as white men do not often hear--such as I hope no one will ever hear again, even from those places.

"Pedro was my Visayan servant, a good worker and a likable fellow in every way. He came to me one Sunday morning in great distress. His twin brother had been dragged into the tribunal that morning by the 'cuadrilleros,' and was at that very moment being flogged. Could I not help him? Would I not go to the Governor and tell him that Pedro would pay his brother's tribute as soon as he could earn the money?

"If course I would. I would gladly do more than that I would pay the money myself and let Pedro earn it afterwards. The man's last wages, I knew, had gone to pay his old father's taxes and his own. His family lived some little distance inland.

"We lost no time in getting to the tribunal. Pedro told me on the way, and I think he told me the truth, that his brother's tax was not rightly due then, else he would have been ready with the money.

"I have always been glad I had Pedro wait outside the door of the government house.

"His brother was bound upon the whipping bench, his body bare to the waist. A row of stripes which ran diagonally across his bare back from hip to shoulder showed where each blow of the rattan had cut through skin and flesh so that the blood flowed back to mark its course.

"'Stop!' I cried, rushing forward to where the Governor was standing. 'Stop! I will pay this man's tax. How much is it? Let him up! I'll pay for him.'

"The Governor looked at me a moment, and, excited as I was, I noticed that his face was set in an angry scowl.

"'You can't pay for him, now,' he said. 'No one can pay for him now.'

"'I'll teach them,' he added, a moment later, 'See that!' holding up his left arm, about the wrist of which I saw a handkerchief was bound, fresh stained with blood.

"'Go on!' he cried, to the man with the rod.

"At first I could not find out what had happened. Then a soldier told me.

"The man had been brought in like a snared animal, held by the jungle ropes, each thorn of which was agony. When he had cried out that he was unjustly tortured, the Governor himself had dragged the clinging hooks from out his flesh, and had called him a name which to the Visayan means deathly insult if it be not resented.

"At which Pedro's brother, snatching a knife which was hidden inside his clothing, struck at the Governor and wounded him in the arm, before he could be caught by the soldiers, disarmed, and bound down on the bench.

"And all the time I had been learning this, the blows of the flog-man had been falling, laid on with an artistic cruelty across the other welts.

"I could not bear it. At the risk of destroying my chances to be allowed to finish my work in the island, perhaps even at the risk of putting my own life in danger, I tried once more.

"'Unless you stop,' I cried, 'I will report you to your government.'

"The 'Gobernadorcillo' looked at me a moment, and almost smiled--a smile which showed his teeth at the sides of his mouth.

"'Please yourself.' he said. 'But unless you like what I am doing I would suggest that you step out.'

"The man died that night, in the prison beneath the tribunal.

"I kept my word, and wrote a full account of the whole affair to the Governor-general at Manila. It was weeks before I received a curt note in reply, saying that the general government made it a rule not to interfere with the local jurisdiction of its subordinates.

"Pedro never spoke to me of his brother's death but once. There was in his nature much of the same grim courage which had enabled his brother to bear the awful pain of that day upon the whipping bench without a cry.

"'Senor,' Pedro said one day, quite suddenly, 'I would not have you think me a coward, that I do not avenge my brother's death. I would have killed the Governor at once, or now, or any day, openly, glad to have him know how and why, and glad to die for the deed, only that now there is no one but me left to care for my old father, It is not that I am a coward, but that I wait.'

"I expect that I should have felt myself in duty bound to expostulate with him, upon harbouring such a state of mind as that, regardless of what my own private opinion in the matter may have been, had it not been that before I could decide just what I wanted to say, a man had come to my house to tell me that the mail steamer from Manila, which came to the island only once in two months was come in sight.

"The coming of that particular steamer was of special interest to me, as it was to bring me a stock of supplies; and Pedro and I went down to the dock at once.

"I remember that invoice in particular, because it brought me a supply of chloroform, a drug, which I had been out of, and for which I was anxiously waiting. Two months before, a native from far back in the forest had brought me a fine live ape. I could not keep him alive,--that is not after I left the island,--and I wanted his skin and skeleton for the museum, but I hated to mar the beauty of the specimen by a wound. That night with Pedro's help I put him quietly out of the way, with the help of the chloroform.

"Afterwards the thought came back to me that as we took away the cone and cotton, when I was sure the animal was dead, Pedro said, 'Senor, how like a man he looks.'

"Several weeks later the residents of Dumaguete were thrown into intense if subdued excitement by the news that the Gobernadorcillo was dead. Apparently well as usual the night before, he had been found dead in hie bed in the morning, in the room in the 'gobierno' in which he slept. If he had been killed on the street, or found stabbed, or shot, in his room, the commotion would not have been so great. Such things as that had happened in Negros more than once, to other officials. But this man was simply dead.

"The 'teniente primero,' who, as next in authority, took charge of affairs upon the death of his superior, sent a man during the day to ask me if I would come to the tribunal. He was a very decent man, or would have been, I think, under a different executive. Naturally he was anxious, under the circumstances, as to his own standing with the authorities at Cebu, and he asked for my evidence, if necessary, as that of one of the few foreigners in the place.

"In company with him I visited the late governor's room in the 'gobierno.' It was a large room, like all of those in the palace, as the executive mansion was sometimes called, built upon the ground floor, and having several lattice windows. A soldier was on duty in the room. As we were coming out, this man came to us, and saluting the 'teniente,' handed him a small tin can, saying, 'A servant cleaning the room, found this.'

"The 'teniente' looked at the can curiously, and then, handing it to me, asked me if I knew what it was.

"'It is a can in which a kind of strong liquor sometimes comes,' I said. Then I unscrewed the top. The can was empty, but I showed him that there was still a strong and pungent odor which lingered in it. The explanation satisfied him. The late governor had been known to be a man who had more than a passing liking for strong liquors.

"I did not feel called upon to explain that the can was a chloroform can, and that no one in the place but myself had any like it.

"When I went home, though, and counted my stock, I found, as I had expected, that it was one can short; and that the cone and cotton which I had used for giving the drug had been replaced by one freshly made.

"I did not think it necessary, either, to impart the result of my investigations to the authorities, or to suggest to them any suspicions which might have been roused in my own mind.

"Even if there had not been very decided personal reasons why I would better not, unless I was obliged to, I had in mind that letter of a few months before, when these same authorities had informed me of their policy of non-interference in local affairs.

"Moreover, I could not but remember what I had seen that day, when the man now dead had said to me, 'I'll teach them.' If his teachings had been effectual, had I any reason to criticise?"

TOLD AT THE CLUB

Speaking of 'anting-anting,'" said a man at the club House on the bank of the Pasig river, in Manila, one evening, "I have had an experience in that line myself which was rather striking."

An American officer at the club that evening had just been telling us about a native prisoner captured by his command sometime before in one of the smaller islands, who, when searched, had been found to be wearing next his skin a sort of undershirt on which was roughly painted a crude map of certain of the islands of the archipelago.

This shirt, it seemed, the officer went on to explain, the man regarded as a powerful "anting-anting," which would be able to protect him from injury in any of the islands represented on it. That he had been taken alive, instead of having been killed in the fight in which he was captured, the man firmly believed to be due to the fact that he was wearing the shirt at the time. A native servant in the employ of one of the officers of the company had explained later that such an "anting-anting" as this was highly prized, and that it increased in value with its age. Only certain "wise men" had the right to add a new island to the number of those painted on the garment, and before this could be done the wearer of the shirt must have performed some great deed of valour in that particular island. The magic garment was worn only in time of war, or when danger was known to threaten, and was bequeathed from father to son, or, sometimes, changed ownership in a less peaceful way.

"What was the experience which you have referred to?" I finally asked the man who had spoken, when he did not seem inclined to go on of his own accord.

The man hesitated a moment before he replied to my question, and something in his manner then, or perhaps when he did speak, made me feel as if he was sorry that he had spoken at all.

"It is a story I do not like to tell," he said, and then added hastily a little later, as if in explanation, "I mean I do not like to tell it because I cannot help feeling, when I do tell it, that people do not believe me to be telling the truth.

"Some years ago," he continued, "I went down to the island of Mindoro to hunt 'timarau,' one of the few large wild animals of the islands--a queer beast, half way between a wild hog and a buffalo.

"I hired as a guide and tracker, a wiry old Mangyan native who seemed to have an instinct for finding a 'timarau' trail and following it where my less skillful eyes could see nothing but undisturbed forest, and who also seemed to have absolutely no fear, a thing which was even more remarkable than his skill, since the natives as a general thing are notably timid about getting in the way of an angry 'timarau.' As a matter of fact I did not blame them so very much for this, after I had had one experience myself in trying to dodge the wild charge of one of these animals infuriated by a bullet which I had sent into his body.

"Perico, though,--that was the old man's name,--never seemed to have the least fear.

"I was surprised, then, one morning when the weather and forest were both in prime condition for a Hunt, to have my guide flatly refuse to leave our camp. Nothing which I could say or do had the least influence upon him. I reasoned, and threatened, and coaxed, and swore, but all to no effect.

"When I asked him why he would not go,--what was the matter,--was he ill? he did not seem to be inclined to answer at first, except to say that he was not ill; but finally, later in the day, he explained to me that he had had a 'warning' that it would not be safe for him to go hunting that day; that his life would be in danger if he did go.

"Perico had been about the islands much more than most of the men of his tribe. He had even been to Manila once or twice, and so not only knew much more about the world than most Mangyans did, but had also picked up enough of the Spanish language so that he could speak it fairly well. In this way he was able to tell me, finally, how the 'warning' had come to him, and why he put so much confidence in it. He also told me this was why he had been so brave about the hunting before. He knew that he was not in any danger so long as he was not forewarned. When he had been warned he avoided the danger by staying quietly in camp, or in some place of safety.

"Even after he had told me as much as this, Perico would not explain to me just how the 'warning' had come, until, at last, he said that 'the stone' had told him.

"This stone, he said, was a wonderful 'anting-anting' which had been in his family for many years. His father had given it to him, and his grandfather had given it to his father.

"Once, many, many years before, there had been an ancestor of his who had been famous through all the tribe for his goodness and wisdom. This man, when very old, had one day taken shelter under a tree from a furious storm. While he was there fire from the sky had come down upon the tree, and when the storm was over the man was found dead. Grasped tightly in one of the dead man's hands was found a small flat stone, smooth cut and polished, which no one of his family had ever seen him have before. Naturally the stone was looked upon as a precious 'anting-anting,' sent down from the sky, and was religiously watched until its mysterious properties were understood, and it was learned that it had the power to forewarn its owner against impending evil. When danger threatened its owner, Perico said, the stone glowed at night with a strange light which he believed was due to its celestial origin. At all other times it was a plain dull stone.

"The night before, for the first time in months, the stone had flashed forth its strange light; and as a result its owner would do nothing which would place him in any danger which he could avoid.

"I thought of all the strange stories I had read and heard of meteors falling from the sky, and of phosphoric rocks, and of little known chemical elements which were mysteriously sensitive to certain atmospheric conditions, and wondered if Perico's stone could be any of these. All my requests to be allowed to see the wonderful stone, however, proved fruitless, Perico was obdurate. There was a tradition that it must not be looked at by daylight, he said, and that the eyes of no one but its owner should gaze upon it.

"And so, for eight beautiful days of magnificent hunting weather, that aggravating heathen stone kept us idle there in the midst of the Mindoro forest. I could not go alone, and Perico simply would not go so long as the stone glowed at night, as, he informed me each morning, it had done. It was in vain that I fretted, and offered him twice, and four times, and, finally--with a desire to see how much in earnest the man really was--ten times his regular wages if he would go with me for just one hunt. He simply would not stir out of the camp, until, on the morning of the ninth day, he met me with a cheerful face, and said, 'Senor, we will hunt today. The stone is black once more.'

"And hunt we did,--that day, and many more--for the stone remained accommodatingly dark after that--and we had good luck, too.

"When I came back to Manila I brought Perico with me. He had begun to have serious trouble with one of his eyes, which threatened to render him unable to follow the work of hunting of which he was so fond. I tried to make him believe that this was the danger of which he claimed he had been warned by the stone, but he would not agree to this, saying that his 'anting-anting' always foretold only a violent death, or some serious bodily injury. In Manila I had him see that Jose Rizal who afterwards became so prominent in the political troubles of the islands, and who had such a tragic later history. Senor Rizal, who had studied in Europe, was a skillful oculist, and an operation which he performed on Perico's eye was entirely successful. I kept the old man with me until he was fully recovered, and then sent him back to his native island. Before he went, he thanked me over and over again for what I had done, and kept telling me that some time he would pay me for it all.

"I laughed at him, at first, not thinking what he meant, until, just before he was to go to the boat, he clasped my hand in both his, and said, 'Senor, I have no children to leave the "anting anting" of my family to. When I die, it shall be yours.'

"I would have laughed again, then, had it not been that the poor old fellow was so much in earnest that it would have been cruel. As it was, I thanked him, and told him I hoped he would live many years to be the guardian of the stone, and to be guarded by it himself.

"After Perico had gone, I forgot all about him. Imagine my surprise, then, when a little more than a year afterward, I received a small packet from a man whom I knew in Calupan, the seaport of Mindoro, and a letter, telling me that my old guide was dead, and that during the illness which had preceded his death he had arranged to have the packet which came with the letter sent to me.

"The package and letter reached me one morning. Of course I knew what Perico had sent me, and, foolish as it may seem, a bit of tenderness for the old man's genuine faith in his talisman made me, mindful of his admonition that the stone must not be exposed to the light of day, restrain my curiosity to open the package until I was in my rooms that night. What I found, when at last I held the mysterious charm in my hands, was a smooth, dark, flint-like disc, about an inch and a half in diameter, and perhaps half an inch in thickness.

"Whatever the stone might have done for its former owners, or might do for me at some other time, it certainly had no errand to perform that night. It was just a plain, dark stone, and no matter how long I looked at it, or in what position, it did not change its appearance.

"Finally, half provoked with myself at my thoughts, I put the stone into a little cabinet in which were other curious souvenirs of my travels in the islands, and forgot it.

"Two years after that it became necessary for me to go to Europe. I had taken passage on one of the regular steamers from Manila to Hong Kong, and was to re-ship from there. As I expected to return in a few months, I did not give up my lodgings, but before I started I packed away much of my stuff for safe keeping. As I was busy at the office during the day, I did the most of this packing in the evenings. In the course of this work I came to the little cabinet of which I have spoken, and threw it open in order to stuff it with cotton, so that the contents would not rattle about when moved."

The man who was telling the story stopped at this point so long that we who sat there in the smoking room of the Club listening to him were afraid he was not going to continue. At last he said:--

"This is the part of the story which I do not like to tell.

"On the black velvet lining of the cabinet, surrounded by the jumble of curios among which it had been tossed, lay old Perico's stone,--not the plain, dark stone which I had put there, but a faintly glowing circle of lustrous light.

"I shut the lid of the cabinet down, locked the box, and put the key in my pocket. But I did no more packing that night. I came down here to the Club, and stayed as long as I could get anybody to stay with me, and talked of everything under the sun except the one thing which I was all the time thinking about.

"The next day I told myself I was a fool, and crazy into the bargain, and that my eyes had deceived me. And then, in spite of all this, when I went home at night

I could hardly wait for dusk to come that I might open the cabinet.

"The stone lay on the velvet, just as the night before, as if it were a thing on fire!

"I said to myself that I would have some common sense, and would exercise my will power; and went on with my packing with furious energy. But I did not put the cabinet where I could not get at it.

"The boat for Hong Kong on which I had taken passage was to sail the next night. I finished my work, said good bye to my acquaintances, and went on board. Fifteen minutes before the steamer sailed I had my luggage tumbled from her deck back on to the wharf, and came ashore, swearing at myself for a fool, and knowing that I would be well laughed at and quizzed for my fickleness by every one who knew me."

The man stopped again. After a little, one of the men who had been listening to him said, in a voice which sounded strangely softened:--

"I remember. That was the ----," calling the name of a steamer which brought to us all the recollection of one of the most awful sea tragedies of those terrible tropic waters, where sometimes sea and wind seem to be in league to buffet and destroy.

"Yes," said the man who had told the story. "No person who sailed on board of her that night was ever seen again; and only bits of wreckage on one of the northern reefs gave any hint of her fate."

PEARLS OF SULU

Now and then people comment upon the odd style of a charm which I wear upon my watch chain. The charm is a plain, gold sphere, and is, I acknowledge, a trifle too large to be in good taste.

If those who ask me about the charm are people whom I care to trust, I sometimes open the globe--it has a secret spring--and show them hidden away inside, a single pearl, so large and perfect that no one who has ever seen it has failed to marvel at its beauty. If they ask me why I wear so regal a gem, and where I got it, I tell them that I am not quite sure that the jewel is mine, and that if I ever find the person who seems to have a better right to it than I, I shall give it up. Meanwhile I like to wear the locket where I can sometimes look at the pearl, since it is a reminder of what I think was the strangest adventure I ever had in the Philippine Islands. And I had many queer experiences there during the years I have journeyed up and down the archipelago in one capacity and another.

One summer when I was collecting specimens for a great European museum, I was living on the southeastern shore of the island of Palawan. Or rather I was living above, or beside the shore of the island; I don't know which word would best describe the location of my house, which, however, one could hardly say was on the island.

The Moros who live on that side of the island which is washed by the Sulu Sea, and who ostensibly depend upon pearl fishing for a living, and really lived by their high-handed deeds of piracy against their neighbors and mankind in general, inhabit odd houses which are built on stout posts driven into the sand at the edge of the sea. The walls of the houses are woven of bamboo, and the roofs are thatched, like those of nearly all the native habitations, but the location is unique. When the tide is high, the surface of the water--fortunately the village is built over a sheltered bay--comes to within two feet beneath the floors of the houses, and the inhabitants go ashore in cockle-shell boats. When the tide is low the foundation posts rise out of the mud and sand, and the people go inland on foot, dodging piles of seaweed and similar debris, left by the receding waves.

It was one of these houses that I hired, and in it set up my household belongings while I was at work in that part of Palawan.

The location had many advantages, for at that time I was principally engaged in collecting corals, sponges, shell fish and similar salt-water specimens. The natives brought me boat loads of such material, for once in their lives, at least, working for honest wages. I sorted over the stuff they brought, on a platform built out in front of my house, and disposed of the mass of refuse in the easiest way imaginable, merely by shoving it off the edge of the platform into the water, where the tide washed it out to sea.

Then, too, this keeping house over the water brought a blessed relief from the invasion of one's home by snakes, rats, ants and all the vermin of that kind which makes Philippine housekeeping on the land a burden to the flesh, while I did not foresee at first that the very water which protected me from these dangers might make possible the secret incursions of larger creatures. The disadvantage of this semi-marine style of architecture, as I looked at it, was that some night a big tidal wave might come along, chasing a frolicsome earthquake, and bearing my house and myself along with it, leave us hanging high and dry in the tops of some clump of palm trees half a dozen miles inland.

So far as the Moros were concerned, I got along all right with them. They knew, in the first place, that I had the authority of the Spanish government to do about what I chose in Palawan, and although they cared not one ripple of the Sulu Sea for the authority of Spain when it could not be enforced by force of arms, they did respect my arsenal of weapons and the skill with which I one day shot down a crazy "tulisane" of their tribe who had started to run amuck, and by the shot saved the lives of no one knew how many of them. This, and my doctoring back to health two of their number who were ill, made us very good friends, and I could not have asked for more willing helpers, or more able, especially Poljensio.

It was not for many weeks after I had left Palawan for good, that I came to understand that Poljensio may have had a double reason for his willingness, which at the time I little suspected.

I remember very well the first time I saw the fellow. It was the day of the "ma-casla" festival. Up to that time I had found no Moro who would work steadily as my helper. Whatever men I hired, although satisfactory while they worked, would eventually have something else to do, either pearl fishing, or hunting, or long trips seaward in their proas, they said for fishing, but I thought, and found later I had thought rightly, for robbery. Even Poljensio used to claim time, now and then, when he said the conditions of the water and weather were favorable for finding pearl oysters, to go and dive for those lottery-ticket-like bivalves.

To tell the truth I did not blame the men so very much for turning pirates, after I came really to understand the conditions connected with the pearl fisheries.

The pearl oysters live at the bottom of such deep water, and are so hard to get, that I have often seen a man come up from his search for them with blood running from his ears and nose, the result of staying down so long. Of course such things as divers' suits, and air pumps, were unknown there. The men stripped their slim, brown bodies naked, and went over the side of the boat with no apparatus except their two hands and a sharp knife to use against the sharks. Sometimes the men never came back, and then we knew the knife had not been quick enough. Poljen-sio had a row of scars on one leg, where a shark had bitten him, years before, which made the leg look as if it had been between the bars of a giant's broiling iron.

Then, after the forces of nature had been overcome, as if they alone were not bad enough, the representatives of the government, the "Gobernadorcillo," had to be reckoned with; and he was worse than all the rest.

The pearl fisheries of Palawan were the property of the Sultan of Sulu. At least up to that time that monarch had been able to maintain an ownership in them which allowed him to claim all of the pearls above a certain size. All that the div-ers got for their risk and labor were the small pearls and the shells. Fortunately for them most of the shells had a market value for cutting into cameos, and for inlay work, and the Chinese dealers who came to Palawan bought them, as well as the pearls.

It was the business of the "Gobernadorcillo" to watch the divers, and take from them all the pearls large enough to become the perquisite of the Sultan. The men were allowed to go out to the water over the oyster beds only on certain days, and then the Sultan's representative went with them, and sat in his boat to keep watch that no shells were opened there. After the boats had returned to the land every oyster shell was opened under his watchful eye, and every large pearl was claimed. Of course it was only rarely that an oyster held a pearl, more rarely still that the gem was a large one. When they did find a big one it always made me feel sorry to see the poor fellow, who had worked so hard for it, have to give the prize up to go, no doubt, to deck some one of the four hundred wives of the ruler who lived across the Sulu Sea.

Poljensio was one of the best of the divers. It was at the "macasla" festival, as I have said, that I first noticed him. For a month the natives had talked about "macasla," and this, with what I had heard about it before, made me anxious to see the performance. So far as I knew I was the first American who had ever had the opportunity. It is only rarely that the festival can be kept, because its success depends upon the possession by the natives of the berries of a certain shrub, which must be in just such a stage of ripeness to have the requisite power. The plant on which the berries grow is not at all common. In this case it was necessary to send a long way into a distant part of the island to get the berries.

The "macasla" festival is really a great fishing expedition, in which every man, woman and child who lives near the village where it is held takes part. The berries are the essential element in a great mass, composed of various ingredients mixed together; just the same as a bit of yeast put into a pan of bread leavens the whole lot. One very old man was said to be the only person near there who understood just how to make the mixture. A large log which had been hollowed out and used at one time for a canoe, was utilized as a trough to make the mixture in. The mass was mixed up in the afternoon and left to ferment overnight. When he had it ready the old man covered the canoe with banana leaves and forbade any one to go near it until the next morning. I saw several different kinds of vegetable substances crushed up, to be put into the canoe, besides the berries; and at last a quantity of wood ashes were added.

The next morning every one was out early, as it was necessary to begin operations when the tide was at its very lowest point. Every one about the village was on hand, each person bringing a loosely woven wicker basket, into which was put a small quantity of the mixture from the old log canoe. When all had been provided with this they walked out as far as they could go, to where the tide was just turning. Then, waiting until the incoming water had passed them on its way inland, the natives, formed in a long line parallel with the shore, dropped their baskets into the water and shook them to and fro until all of the "macasla" had been washed out through the loose wicker work.

In about ten minutes the effect of the mixture began to be seen. The smaller fish were affected first, and began to come to the top of the water, as if for air. Very soon they were followed by the larger ones, and soon the water seemed filled with them. They would come to the top of the water, turn on one side, flop about a little as if intoxicated, and then sink helplessly to the bottom, where, the water being nowhere very deep, it was easy to see them and capture them. The natives secured basket after basket full, getting some so large that they could not carry them in their baskets. These they would disable with a "machete" and then tow ashore. The fish did not eat the "macasla." It seemed simply to have impregnated the water, making a solution too powerful for them to withstand. They were not killed by its effects, but acted as if they were drunk. Those which the natives did not capture soon recovered and swam away as briskly as ever. Before they were able to do this though, the natives had secured more than enough food to last them as long as it would remain eatable.

Of course I found the miscellaneous harvest of sea animals which the "macasla" brought in most interesting, and secured a good many valuable specimens. Inasmuch as I had contributed very materially to the feast which was to take place that night, and which lasted all night long, the people let me wade about among the strangely helpless creatures and have a first pick of such as I wanted. I had noticed Poljensio running about, as one of the strongest and most agile of all the men in the water, and when he came near me once, when my basket was heavy, I offered to hire him to help me, although I had little idea that any one would work for wages at such a time. Quite to my surprise he seemed willing, and joined me in what I was doing. I learned afterwards that having no family to provide for he was not so much in need of profiting by the fish harvest as most of the men were. He had worked in the water all his life, and knew more about the habits of some of the creatures we caught than I did. When we came to go to my house, and he saw the specimens I had preserved there, he seemed to take a more intelligent interest in them than any other man I had ever had, and I was glad to be able to hire him to work for me all of the time, barring the few days he reserved for pearl fishing.

The season which followed proved to be an unusually successful one for the divers. The crop of oysters was large, and many pearls were found. The gems which were to go to the Sultan were superb, and there would be enough of them to make a truly royal necklace.

One night about six months after the "macasla" festival I woke suddenly from a sound sleep, with that strange feeling which sometimes comes to one at night, that I was not alone. While I lay listening and peering into the darkness of the room in which I slept, I heard a soft splash in the water beneath me, such as a big fish might have made if he had come to the surface, and diving back had struck the water with his tail. It had been high tide soon after midnight, and the water was not more than three or four feet beneath me. I listened a long time, but could hear nothing more, and finally went to sleep again, deciding that the splash I had heard had been made by a shark, and that some noise which he had made before that had been what had roused me.

Any further thought of my disturbance which I might have had was driven from my mind in the morning, when I came out and found the community in a state of violent commotion.

The "gobierno," the house in which the "Gobernadorcillo" lived, had been robbed in the night, and a bag containing about half the Sultan's pearls was gone. The government official, along with several other residents, lived on shore. The houses which, like mine, were built over the water, were generally inhabited by the divers and their families.

The voice of the "Gobernadorcillo" was not the only one raised in lamentation that morning, by any means, for he had very promptly begun a search for the missing jewels by beating his servants and every one connected with the official residence, within an inch of their lives. When this did not produce the pearls he extended the process to such other unfortunate residents of the town as fell under his suspicion. I really think the only thing which kept him from killing a few of the wretches was the fear that he might by some chance include the thief in the number, and thus destroy all hope of getting back the stolen gems.

No man, woman or child was allowed to leave the village, and so thorough was the system by which one of those deputy tax collectors kept track of his people, that he knew every one by name, and knew just where each one should be found. His superiors required a certain sum of money from each tax collector. They did not care in the smallest degree where or how he got the money, but a certain amount he must turn in at stated times, or else be put in prison and have other unpleasant things done to him. So it stood the "Gobernadorcillo" in good stead to know who his people were, and where they were, and how much each person could be made to pay.

As soon as his arm was rested from the beating he had given the suspected natives the official began a personal search of each house in the village. The native houses are so simple, and their stock of furniture so small, that it was no great task to make a thorough inspection of the entire place. What little furniture each house had was outside of it when the examination of that house was completed. It was fortunate for the people who lived in the houses built over the water that their homes were visited at low tide, for in the state of the examiner's temper when he visited them I think their effects would have gone out into the sea just as quickly as they went out on to the sand.

Even my house came under the terms of the universal edict, although my things were not used so harshly as were those of the natives, which was fortunate for me, for I had hundreds of specimens packed, and many more ready to pack, which I should have been very sorry indeed to have had dumped out of doors.

My relations with the Governor had always been pleasant. He really was quite as good a man as any one in his place could be expected to be. We had gotten along very well together, and I was glad now that this was so. When he came to my house he contented himself with looking through the part of the building where the native servant who cooked for me worked and lived. Poljensio slept at home, and spent only the daytime at my house. The search of that part of the establishment over, the worried official sat down in my work room to rest for a few minutes, cool himself off, and bewail the fate which had brought him such ill luck. Poljensio, who was washing sponges on the platform outside, and had for this reason not been at his brother's house, where he slept, when that domicile was searched, was called in, and while his official master rested, was made to strip himself stark naked, and turn his few slight garments--the clothing of a Moro is always an uncertain quantity--

inside out to show that nothing was hidden therein.

Knowing the place so well as I did, and the means at the command of the "Gobernadorcillo," I could not for the life of me see how any one who had stolen the pearls could keep them, or hide them, for that matter, unless they had been thrown back into the sea again.

So far as the governor himself was concerned he would not suffer from the loss. The yearly crop of pearls was not like the money tax, a stated sum, nor could the Sultan enforce his claims as did the Spanish government. His title to the fisheries was too slight for it to be policy for him to make trouble. Besides that, Sulu was so far away that its ruler might never hear that this year's crop had been larger than usual. Not all the gems had been taken. The governor could turn over what had been left him, and it was not at all likely that any questions would be asked. In fact, if it had not been for his evident concern, which I did not believe him clever enough to have simulated, I would almost have believed he had stolen the pearls himself. He certainly was indefatigable in his attempts to find the missing property. Not a native left the village for any purpose that his clothing and his boat, if he was going out upon the water, were not inspected.

My own stay in Palawan was nearly ended at the time, and it was not long after that before I had completed my collections, packed my specimens, and was ready to go. Poljensio had agreed to go with me as far as Manila, to handle my freight and baggage, and to help me there about repacking and shipping my specimens. On my going to Europe he was to return to Palawan.

When I was ready to go, and had my luggage in shape to be sent on board the sail boat which was to take me to a port visited by the monthly steamer to Manila, I wondered if the "Gobernadorcillo" would let me go. He proved very obliging, however, shook hands, and hoped I would have a pleasant voyage. Poljensio, though, had to submit to the usual ordeal of having his clothing searched. Luggage he had none, so he was not troubled in that respect.

I had planned to stop in Hong Kong a month on my way to Europe. On the morning of the day that I was to leave there I was surprised to receive a package by one of the local English expresses of the city, and more surprised to find that the package contained a small box of specimens which had been missing when I had repacked my property at Manila. The specimens in this box were particularly choice ones, and their loss had been as annoying as it had been unaccountable. The pleasure which I felt in getting them back, though, was nothing compared to my amazement when I found along with the package another small one containing a letter from Poljensio.

The letter, if I had chosen to put it among my specimens, would have ranked, I am sure, among the greatest curiosities of the whole collection. Poljensio was not a scholar. His accomplishments lay in the line of diving and swimming; in gathering pearls, and such things as that. He never would have wasted his time in struggling with pen and paper, now, if the nature of the correspondence had not been such that he could not safely entrust it to any one else; and the full comprehension of the remarkable document, written in the mingled native and Spanish languages, with which he had favored me, was not vouchsafed to me at the first reading, or the second.

Translated, and made as nearly coherent as possible, it ran about like this:

"I stole the pearls. I only took half, so not too much" (scrimmage, fuss, row, trouble,--the native word he used meant no one of these exactly, and yet included them all) "would be made. I was tired of working so hard, and the sharks, and not getting anything for it but shells. I made up my mind I would do it soon after I went to work for you. I went diving after that only that I be not suspected. I knew all of us native people would be searched, but I thought he would pass you by. So that night, after I had got the pearls, I swam out to your house, climbed up through the floor, and hid the bag in a place where I would know. Then, one day, when I packed a fine big shell, I hid the bag in it, and marked the box. When we got to Manila I stole the box. I sorrow to make you this bad time, but have no other way. I take good care of box, though, after I take pearls out, to bring it here with me, and now I send it back. I sell all the pearls here but one, to China merchant, for money enough to make me always a rich man. I don't think I go back to Palawan. One pearl I save back, and send you with this letter, to remember by it Poljensio."

That was what was in the package with the letter. The pearl he had saved; this one which I wear.

As I said in the first place, I am ready give it up when I can find a man who has a better claim to it than I have. My right of ownership in the gem is not, I confess, very substantial; but whose is it?

It was not the "Gobernadorcillo's," for he was only an agent; and besides that he left Palawan not long after I did, as I have found out by inquiry, and I cannot learn where he now is.

The Sultan of Sulu who reigned then is dead, and if the gem belonged to him it did not belong to his successor; for the friends of the first ruler declared that the man who gained the throne after him was a false claimant. Should I send it to the dead man's heirs? He had no son, and one can hardly divide one pearl among four hundred widows.

Only Poljensio is left, and his claim, even if I could find him, I fear would be counted hardly legal. Quite likely he would not take it back, even if I found him; and sometimes, when I reflect upon what would probably have happened to me if the bag of stolen pearls had been found by any chance in my house, I am not sure that I should feel like offering the gem to him.

The Codes Of Hammurabi And Moses
W. W. Davies

QTY

The discovery of the Hammurabi Code is one of the greatest achievements of archaeology, and is of paramount interest, not only to the student of the Bible, but also to all those interested in ancient history...

Religion   **ISBN:** *1-59462-338-4*   **Pages:132**

MSRP $12.95

The Theory of Moral Sentiments
Adam Smith

QTY

This work from 1749. contains original theories of conscience amd moral judgment and it is the foundation for systemof morals.

Philosophy **ISBN:** *1-59462-777-0*   **Pages:536**

MSRP $19.95

Jessica's First Prayer
Hesba Stretton

QTY

In a screened and secluded corner of one of the many railway-bridges which span the streets of London there could be seen a few years ago, from five o'clock every morning until half past eight, a tidily set-out coffee-stall, consisting of a trestle and board, upon which stood two large tin cans, with a small fire of charcoal burning under each so as to keep the coffee boiling during the early hours of the morning when the work-people were thronging into the city on their way to their daily toil...

Childrens   **ISBN:** *1-59462-373-2*

Pages:84

MSRP $9.95

My Life and Work
Henry Ford

QTY

Henry Ford revolutionized the world with his implementation of mass production for the Model T automobile. Gain valuable business insight into his life and work with his own auto-biography... "We have only started on our development of our country we have not as yet, with all our talk of wonderful progress, done more than scratch the surface. The progress has been wonderful enough but..."

Biographies/   **ISBN:** *1-59462-198-5*

Pages:300

MSRP $21.95

The Art of Cross-Examination
Francis Wellman

QTY

I presume it is the experience of every author, after his first book is published upon an important subject, to be almost overwhelmed with a wealth of ideas and illustrations which could readily have been included in his book, and which to his own mind, at least, seem to make a second edition inevitable. Such certainly was the case with me; and when the first edition had reached its sixth impression in five months, I rejoiced to learn that it seemed to my publishers that the book had met with a sufficiently favorable reception to justify a second and considerably enlarged edition. ..

Reference   ISBN: *1-59462-647-2*

Pages:412

MSRP $19.95

On the Duty of Civil Disobedience
Henry David Thoreau

QTY

Thoreau wrote his famous essay, On the Duty of Civil Disobedience, as a protest against an unjust but popular war and the immoral but popular institution of slave-owning. He did more than write—he declined to pay his taxes,   and was hauled off to gaol in consequence. Who can say how much this refusal of his hastened the end of the war and of slavery ?

Law   ISBN: *1-59462-747-9*

Pages:48

MSRP $7.45

Dream Psychology Psychoanalysis for Beginners
Sigmund Freud

QTY

Sigmund Freud, born Sigismund Schlomo Freud (May 6, 1856 - September 23, 1939), was a Jewish-Austrian neurologist and psychiatrist who co-founded the psychoanalytic school of psychology. Freud is best known for his theories of the unconscious mind, especially involving the mechanism of repression; his redefinition of sexual desire as mobile and directed towards a wide variety of objects; and his therapeutic techniques, especially his understanding of transference in the therapeutic relationship and the presumed value of dreams as sources of insight into unconscious desires.

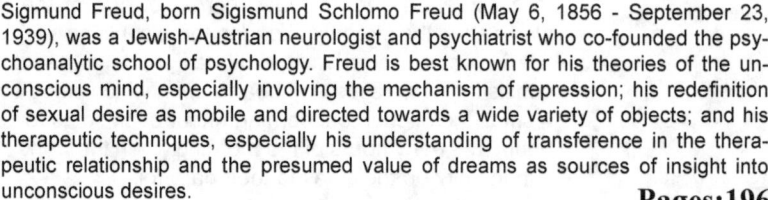

Psychology   ISBN: *1-59462-905-6*

Pages:196

MSRP $15.45

The Miracle of Right Thought
Orison Swett Marden

QTY

Believe with all of your heart that you will do what you were made to do. When the mind has once formed the habit of holding cheerful, happy, prosperous pictures, it will not be easy to form the opposite habit. It does not matter how improbable or how far away this realization may see, or how dark the prospects may be, if we visualize them as best we can, as vividly as possible, hold tenaciously to them and vigorously struggle to attain them, they will gradually become actualized, realized in the life. But a desire, a longing without endeavor, a yearning abandoned or held indifferently will vanish without realization.

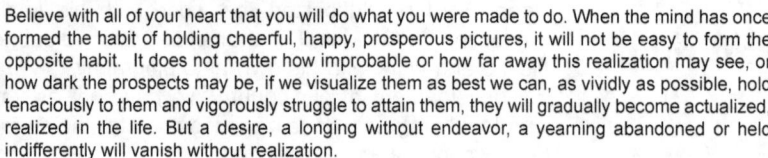

Self Help   ISBN: *1-59462-644-8*

Pages:360

MSRP $25.45

QTY

The Rosicrucian Cosmo-Conception Mystic Christianity *by Max Heindel*   ISBN: 1-59462-188-8   **$38.95**
The Rosicrucian Cosmo-conception is not dogmatic, neither does it appeal to any other authority than the reason of the student. It is: not controversial, but is: sent forth in the, hope that it may help to clear...   *New Age/Religion Pages 646*

Abandonment To Divine Providence *by Jean-Pierre de Caussade*   ISBN: 1-59462-228-0   **$25.95**
"The Rev. Jean Pierre de Caussade was one of the most remarkable spiritual writers of the Society of Jesus in France in the 18th Century. His death took place at Toulouse in 1751. His works have gone through many editions and have been republished...   *Inspirational/Religion Pages 400*

Mental Chemistry *by Charles Haanel*   ISBN: 1-59462-192-6   **$23.95**
Mental Chemistry allows the change of material conditions by combining and appropriately utilizing the power of the mind. Much like applied chemistry creates something new and unique out of careful combinations of chemicals the mastery of mental chemistry...   *New Age Pages 354*

The Letters of Robert Browning and Elizabeth Barret Barrett 1845-1846 vol II   ISBN: 1-59462-193-4   **$35.95**
by Robert Browning and Elizabeth Barrett   *Biographies Pages 596*

Gleanings In Genesis (volume I) *by Arthur W. Pink*   ISBN: 1-59462-130-6   **$27.45**
Appropriately has Genesis been termed "the seed plot of the Bible" for in it we have, in germ form, almost all of the great doctrines which are afterwards fully developed in the books of Scripture which follow...   *Religion/Inspirational Pages 420*

The Master Key *by L. W. de Laurence*   ISBN: 1-59462-001-6   **$30.95**
In no branch of human knowledge has there been a more lively increase of the spirit of research during the past few years than in the study of Psychology, Concentration and Mental Discipline. The requests for authentic lessons in Thought Control, Mental Discipline and...   *New Age/Business Pages 422*

The Lesser Key Of Solomon Goetia *by L. W. de Laurence*   ISBN: 1-59462-092-X   **$9.95**
This translation of the first book of the "Lemegton" which is now for the first time made accessible to students of Talismanic Magic was done, after careful collation and edition, from numerous Ancient Manuscripts in Hebrew, Latin, and French...   *New Age/Occult Pages 92*

Rubaiyat Of Omar Khayyam *by Edward Fitzgerald*   ISBN:1-59462-332-5   **$13.95**
Edward Fitzgerald, whom the world has already learned, in spite of his own efforts to remain within the shadow of anonymity, to look upon as one of the rarest poets of the century, was born at Bredfield, in Suffolk, on the 31st of March, 1809. He was the third son of John Purcell...   *Music Pages 172*

Ancient Law *by Henry Maine*   ISBN: 1-59462-128-4   **$29.95**
The chief object of the following pages is to indicate some of the earliest ideas of mankind, as they are reflected in Ancient Law, and to point out the relation of those ideas to modern thought.   *Religiom/History Pages 452*

Far-Away Stories *by William J. Locke*   ISBN: 1-59462-129-2   **$19.45**
"Good wine needs no bush, but a collection of mixed vintages does. And this book is just such a collection. Some of the stories I do not want to remain buried for ever in the museum files of dead magazine-numbers an author's not unpardonable vanity..."   *Fiction Pages 272*

Life of David Crockett *by David Crockett*   ISBN: 1-59462-250-7   **$27.45**
"Colonel David Crockett was one of the most remarkable men of the times in which he lived. Born in humble life, but gifted with a strong will, an indomitable courage, and unremitting perseverance...   *Biographies/New Age Pages 424*

Lip-Reading *by Edward Nitchie*   ISBN: 1-59462-206-X   **$25.95**
Edward B. Nitchie, founder of the New York School for the Hard of Hearing, now the Nitchie School of Lip-Reading, Inc, wrote "LIP-READING Principles and Practice". The development and perfecting of this meritorious work on lip-reading was an undertaking...   *How-to Pages 400*

A Handbook of Suggestive Therapeutics, Applied Hypnotism, Psychic Science   ISBN: 1-59462-214-0   **$24.95**
by Henry Munro   *Health/New Age/Health/Self-help Pages 376*

A Doll's House: and Two Other Plays *by Henrik Ibsen*   ISBN: 1-59462-112-8   **$19.95**
Henrik Ibsen created this classic when in revolutionary 1848 Rome. Introducing some striking concepts in playwriting for the realist genre, this play has been studied the world over.   *Fiction/Classics/Plays 308*

The Light of Asia *by sir Edwin Arnold*   ISBN: 1-59462-204-3   **$13.95**
In this poetic masterpiece, Edwin Arnold describes the life and teachings of Buddha. The man who was to become known as Buddha to the world was born as Prince Gautama of India but he rejected the worldly riches and abandoned the reigns of power when... Religion/History/Biographies Pages 170

The Complete Works of Guy de Maupassant *by Guy de Maupassant*   ISBN: 1-59462-157-8   **$16.95**
"For days and days, nights and nights, I had dreamed of that first kiss which was to consecrate our engagement, and I knew not on what spot I should put my lips..."   *Fiction/Classics Pages 240*

The Art of Cross-Examination *by Francis L. Wellman*   ISBN: 1-59462-309-0   **$26.95**
Written by a renowned trial lawyer, Wellman imparts his experience and uses case studies to explain how to use psychology to extract desired information through questioning.   *How-to/Science/Reference Pages 408*

Answered or Unanswered? *by Louisa Vaughan*   ISBN: 1-59462-248-5   **$10.95**
Miracles of Faith in China   *Religion Pages 112*

The Edinburgh Lectures on Mental Science (1909) *by Thomas*   ISBN: 1-59462-008-3   **$11.95**
This book contains the substance of a course of lectures recently given by the writer in the Queen Street Hall, Edinburgh. Its purpose is to indicate the Natural Principles governing the relation between Mental Action and Material Conditions...   *New Age/Psychology Pages 148*

Ayesha *by H. Rider Haggard*   ISBN: 1-59462-301-5   **$24.95**
Verily and indeed it is the unexpected that happens! Probably if there was one person upon the earth from whom the Editor of this, and of a certain previous history, did not expect to hear again...   *Classics Pages 380*

Ayala's Angel *by Anthony Trollope*   ISBN: 1-59462-352-X   **$29.95**
The two girls were both pretty, but Lucy who was twenty-one who supposed to be simple and comparatively unattractive, whereas Ayala was credited, as her Bombwhat romantic name might show, with poetic charm and a taste for romance. Ayala when her father died was nineteen...   *Fiction Pages 484*

The American Commonwealth *by James Bryce*   ISBN: 1-59462-286-8   **$34.45**
An interpretation of American democratic political theory. It examines political mechanics and society from the perspective of Scotsman James Bryce   *Politics Pages 572*

Stories of the Pilgrims *by Margaret P. Pumphrey*   ISBN: 1-59462-116-0   **$17.95**
This book explores pilgrims religious oppression in England as well as their escape to Holland and eventual crossing to America on the Mayflower, and their early days in New England...   *History Pages 268*

www.bookjungle.com *email: sales@bookjungle.com fax: 630-214-0564 mail: Book Jungle PO Box 2226 Champaign, IL 61825*

QTY

The Fasting Cure *by Sinclair Upton*   ISBN: *1-59462-222-1*   **$13.95**
In the Cosmopolitan Magazine for May, 1910, and in the Contemporary Review (London) for April, 1910, I published an article dealing with my experi-ences in fasting. I have written a great many magazine articles, but never one which attracted so much attention... New Age/Self Help/Health Pages 164

Hebrew Astrology *by Sepharial*   ISBN: *1-59462-308-2*   **$13.45**
In these days of advanced thinking it is a matter of common observation that we have left many of the old landmarks behind and that we are now pressing forward to greater heights and to a wider horizon than that which represented the mind-content of our progenitors...   Astrology Pages 144

Thought Vibration or The Law of Attraction in the Thought World   ISBN: *1-59462-127-6*   **$12.95**
by William Walker Atkinson   *Psychology/Religion Pages 144*

Optimism *by Helen Keller*   ISBN: *1-59462-108-X*   **$15.95**
Helen Keller was blind, deaf, and mute since 19 months old, yet famously learned how to overcome these handicaps, communicate with the world, and spread her lectures promoting optimism. An inspiring read for everyone...   Biographies/Inspirational Pages 84

Sara Crewe *by Frances Burnett*   ISBN: *1-59462-360-0*   **$9.45**
In the first place, Miss Minchin lived in London. Her home was a large, dull, tall one, in a large, dull square, where all the houses were alike, and all the sparrows were alike, and where all the door-knockers made the same heavy sound...   Childrens/Classic Pages 88

The Autobiography of Benjamin Franklin *by Benjamin Franklin*   ISBN: *1-59462-135-7*   **$24.95**
The Autobiography of Benjamin Franklin has probably been more extensively read than any other American historical work, and no other book of its kind has had such ups and downs of fortune. Franklin lived for many years in England, where he was agent...   Biographies/History Pages 332

Name	
Email	
Telephone	
Address	
City, State ZIP	

☐ **Credit Card**   ☐ **Check / Money Order**

Credit Card Number	
Expiration Date	
Signature	

Please Mail to: Book Jungle
                     PO Box 2226
                     Champaign, IL 61825
or Fax to: 630-214-0564

ORDERING INFORMATION

web*: www.bookjungle.com*
email*: sales@bookjungle.com*
fax*: 630-214-0564*
mail*: Book Jungle PO Box 2226 Champaign, IL 61825*
or PayPal *to sales@bookjungle.com*

Please contact us for bulk discounts

DIRECT-ORDER TERMS

**20% Discount if You Order
Two or More Books**
Free Domestic Shipping!
Accepted: Master Card, Visa,
Discover, American Express

www.ingramcontent.com/pod-product-compliance
Lightning Source LLC
Chambersburg PA
CBHW082015170626
46817CB00009B/3105